Rowe is  1

Praise for No Knight Needed

"*No Knight Needed* is m-a-g-i-c-a-l! Hands down, it is one of the best romances I have read. I can't wait till it comes out and I can tell the world about it." ~*Sharon Stogner, Love Romance Passion*

"*No Knight Needed* is contemporary romance at its best….There was not a moment that I wasn't completely engrossed in the novel, the story, the characters. I very audibly cheered for them and did not shed just one tear, nope, rather bucket fulls. My heart at times broke for them. The narrative and dialogue surrounding these 'tender' moments in particular were so beautifully crafted, poetic even; it was this that had me blubbering. And of course on the flip side of the heart-wrenching events, was the amazing, witty humour….If it's not obvious by now, then just to be clear, I love this book! I would most definitely and happily reread, which is an absolute first for me in this genre." ~*Becky Johnson, Bex 'N' Books*

"*No Knight Needed* is an amazing story of love and life…I literally laughed out loud, cried and cheered…. *No Knight Needed* is a must read and must re-read." ~*Jeanne Stone-Hunter, My Book Addiction Reviews*

Praise for Not Quite Dead

"[Rowe] has penned a winner with *Not Quite Dead*, the first novel in her new NightHunter vampire series...an action-packed, sensual, paranormal romance that will captivate readers from the outset... Brimming with vampires, danger, resurrection, Louisiana bayou, humor, surprising plot twists, fantasy, romance and love, this story is a must-read!" ~ *Romance Junkies:*

❦ ❦ ❦

Praise for Darkness Possessed

"A story that will keep you on the edge of your seat, and characters you won't soon forget!" - Paige Tyler, *USA Today* Bestselling Author of the X-OPS Series

"*Darkness Possessed*…is an action-packed, adrenaline pumping paranormal romance that will keep you on the edge of your seat… Suspense, danger, evil, life threatening situations, magic, hunky Calydons, humor, fantasy, mystery, scorching sensuality, romance, and love – what more could you ask for in a story? Readers – take my advice – do not miss this dark, sexy tale!" *~Romance Junkies*

❦ ❦ ❦

Praise for Darkness Unleashed

"Once more, award winning author Stephanie Rowe pens a winner with *Darkness Unleashed*, the seventh book in her amazing Order of the Blade series…[an] action-packed, sensual story that will keep you perched on the edge of your seat, eagerly turning pages to discover the outcome…one of the best paranormal books I have read this year." *~Dottie, Romancejunkies.com*

❦ ❦ ❦

Praise for Forever in Darkness

"Stephanie Rowe has done it again. The Order Of The Blade series is one of the best urban fantasy/paranormal series I have read. Ian's story held me riveted from page one. It is sure to delight all her fans. Keep them coming!" *~ Alexx Mom Cat's Gateway Book Blog*

❦ ❦ ❦

Praise for Darkness Awakened

"A fast-paced plot with strong characters, blazing sexual tension and sprinkled with witty banter, Darkness Awakened sucked me in and kept me hooked until the very last page." ~ *Literary Escapism*

"Rarely do I find a book that so captivates my attention, that makes me laugh out loud, and cry when things look bad. And the sex, wow! It took my breath away... The pace kept me on the edge of my seat, and turning the pages. I did not want to put this book down... [Darkness Awakened] is a must read." ~ D. Alexx Miller, Alexx Mom Cat's Gateway Book Blog

❦ ❦ ❦

Praise for Darkness Seduced

"[D]ark, edgy, sexy … sizzles on the page...sex with soul shattering connections that leave the reader a little breathless!...Darkness Seduced delivers tight plot lines, well written, witty and lyrical - Rowe lays down some seriously dark and sexy tracks. There is no doubt that this series will have a cult following. " ~ *Guilty Indulgence Book Club*

"I was absolutely enthralled by this book...heart stopping action fueled by dangerous passions and hunky, primal men...If you're looking for a book that will grab hold of you and not let go until it has been totally devoured, look no further than Darkness Seduced."~*When Pen Met Paper Reviews*

❦ ❦ ❦

Praise for Darkness Surrendered

"Book three of the Order of the Blades series is...superbly original and excellent, yet the passion, struggle and the depth of emotion that Ana and Elijah face is so brutal, yet is also pretty awe inspiring. I was swept away by Stephanie's depth of character detail and emotion. I absolutely loved the roller-coaster that Stephanie, Ana and Elijah took me on." ~ *Becky Johnson, Bex 'n' Books!*

"Darkness Surrendered drew me so deeply into the story that I felt

Ana and Elijah's emotions as if they were my own…they completely engulfed me in their story…Ingenious plot turns and edge of your seat suspense…make Darkness Surrendered one of the best novels I have read in years." ~*Tamara Hoffa, Sizzling Hot Book Reviews*

❦ ❦ ❦

Praise for Ice

"*Ice*, by Stephanie Rowe, is a thrill ride!" ~ Lisa Jackson, #1 *New York Times* bestselling author

"Passion explodes even in the face of spiraling danger as Rowe offers a chilling thrill-ride through a vivid--and unforgiving--Alaskan wilderness." ~ Cheyenne McCray, *New York Times* bestselling author

"*Ice* delivers pulse-pounding chills and hot romance as it races toward its exciting climax!" ~ JoAnn Ross, *New York Times* bestselling author

"Stephanie Rowe explodes onto the romantic suspense scene with this edgy, sexy and gripping thriller. From the very first page, the suspense is chilling, and there's enough sizzling passion between the two main characters to melt the thickest arctic ice. Get ready for a tense and dangerous adventure." ~ *Fresh Fiction*

"Stephanie Rowe makes her entry into Romantic Suspense, and what an awesome entry! From the very first pages to the end, heart-stopping danger and passion grab the heart. ... sends shivers down the spine... magnificent... mind-chilling suspense... riveting... A wonderful romance through and through!" ~ *Merrimon Book Reviews*

"[a] thrilling entry into romantic suspense... Rowe comes through with crackling tension as the killer closes in." ~ *Publisher's Weekly*

❦ ❦ ❦

Praise for Chill

"*Chill* is a riveting story of danger, betrayal, intrigue and the healing powers of love... *Chill* has everything a reader needs – death, threats, thefts, attraction and hot, sweet romance." – Jeanne Stone Hunter, *My Book Addiction Reviews*

"Once again Rowe has delivered a story with adrenalin-inducing action, suspense and a dark edged hero that will melt your heart and send a chill down your spine." – Sharon Stogner, *Love Romance Passion*

"*Chill* packs page turning suspense with tremendous emotional impact. Buy a box of Kleenex before you read *Chill*, because you will definitely need it! ...*Chill* had a wonderfully complicated plot, full of twist and turns. " – Tamara Hoffa, *Sizzling Hot Book Reviews*

Acknowledgements

Special thanks to my beta readers, who always work incredibly hard under tight deadlines to get my books read. I appreciate so much your willingness to tell me when something doesn't work! I treasure your help, and I couldn't do this without you. Hugs to you all! Thanks also to the Rockstars, the best buzz team ever!

There are so many to thank by name, more than I could count, but here are those who I want to called out specially for all they did to help this book come to life: Malinda Davis Diehl, Donna Bossert, Leslie Barnes, Kayla Bartley, Alencia Bates Salters, Alyssa Bird, Jean Bowden, Shell Bryce, Kelley Daley Curry, Ashley Cuesta, Denise Fluhr, Sandi Foss, Valerie Glass, Heidi Hoffman, Jeanne Stone, Rebecca Johnson, Dottie Jones, Janet Juengling-Snell, Deb Julienne, Bridget Koan, Felicia Low, Phyllis Marshall, Suzanne Mayer, Erin McRae, Jodi Moore, Ashlee Murphy, Judi Pflughoeft, Carol Pretorius, Kasey Richardson, Caryn Santee, Summer Steelman, Regina Thomas, and Linda Watson.

Special thanks to Michael James Canalas at MJC Imageworks for a wonderful cover. Mom, you're the best. It means so much that you believe in me. I love you. Special thanks also to my amazing, beautiful, special daughter, who I love more than words could ever express. You are my world, sweet girl, in all ways.

Dedication

For Janet Juengling-Snell and Erin Michelle McRae, for all the amazing work and heart that you ladies have spent on launching the Stocktons into the world. You guys ROCK!

A Real Cowboy Knows How to Kiss

A *Wyoming Rebels* Novel

Stephanie Rowe

Chapter 1

Steen Stockton took a deep breath as he stepped outside the prison for the first time in four years. He'd forgotten what freedom tasted like, and he was sort of surprised that he even cared enough to notice the blue sky, the lack of walls, and the fact that he owned himself for the first time in too damn long. He'd thought his soul was dead, but the fact he was actually noticing the warmth of the afternoon sun on his face made him think that maybe he was wrong.

Maybe his soul wasn't dead. At least, not yet. He wasn't sure if that was a good thing, or not.

Being dead was easier.

And now that he was free? He had no idea what to do. He didn't even want to do anything. He simply wanted to walk away, and he didn't care where he ended up.

The long, winding road leading up to the prison was empty, and the parking lot was barren, except for a few staff cars and a shiny silver Mercedes that probably belonged to some hotshot lawyer slumming with the inmates.

Though he'd been officially sprung today, there had been mountains of forms to go through, so actual freedom had come late in the day. He was nothing but an inmate number to them, and he knew it. They didn't care how long it took to get him out the door, but since he'd been paroled, they couldn't keep him inside. Now, he was out.

His body felt like it had been to hell, and had gotten only halfway back. The walk down the steps felt interminable, but he managed to avoid the temptation of using the cement wall of the prison to support himself. Instead, he inched down the stairs, refusing to use the handrail, refusing to be weak.

When he'd been lying in that hospital bed a few months ago, he'd been ready to die. He'd made peace with the uselessness of his life, and he was done. But then somehow, some way, something had changed. He had only vague memories of what his brother's fiancée had said to him when he'd been unconscious, but her words had ripped open something in his gut and dragged him back to the land of the living.

And now, here he was. It had been only a few months since he'd almost died, a hellish period that had involved post-surgical complications and a second surgery. But now he was finally standing outside the prison he'd never thought he'd leave alive.

He was sure she'd said something about a woman. What woman? He needed to ask her. He needed to know, because otherwise, the fact he was still breathing made no sense.

Ignoring the pain from both the stab wound in his left side and the incision bisecting his stomach, he eased down the steps, almost laughing at how out of breath he was. Where was the former star athlete now, eh? The glory days were long past, not that those days had been all that glorious. He knew now they'd just been the setup for the fall.

He'd made it halfway down the flight of stairs, when a shadow moved across his path. Prison instincts flared up, and he stopped fast, his fists going up for protection as he jerked his head up to see who had cut him off.

It was a man in a suit, polished shoes, and a perfect white shirt. His dark hair was flecked with gray, and his smooth shave looked like it had been done in a grooming salon. His face had a few lines on it, but they were the kind of wrinkles a man got from too much stress, not from a lifetime in the sun. He studied Steen silently, evaluating him.

Steen let his fists drop, but his tension didn't lessen. He didn't trust men who paid more for their clothes than average people spent on their cars. He never had trusted people that like, and the last five years had made him even more cynical about human nature.

He was sure the man had never had to fight to save his own life. He almost envied the guy. What would it have been like to grow up having no idea how dirty life could be?

"Steen Stockton, I presume?" The man's voice was cultured and precise.

He knew who he was? Steen's tension rose another notch, but he hid it, giving only a non-committal shrug with one shoulder. "Maybe."

"They said you were getting paroled today."

Steen stiffened, as it occurred to him that the man could be associated with the people who had gotten him thrown into prison in the first place. He immediately raised his chin and relaxed his hands. There was no chance in hell he was going to be goaded into doing anything that could get his ass thrown back in prison. He was done with that. *Done.* "What's it to you?"

The man was unruffled by Steen's surly tone. "I've been waiting all day for you to come out. I wanted to thank you personally."

Steen paused at the unexpected answer. "*Thank* me? For what?"

The man cleared his throat. "I'm sorry. I've been remiss. My name is Thomas Smith." He held out his hand, and Steen reluctantly shook it. No one had shaken his hand in a long, long time.

"Okay," Steen said carefully, still unclear what the man wanted from him. He shifted restlessly, wanting to get away from the building that had trapped him for so long. He had no clue where he was going to go, but that didn't matter. He just wanted to hike down that long driveway and start over.

No, first he was going to find his brother's woman, and ask her what she'd said to him to pull him out of his coma. The words in his head wouldn't connect, and he didn't like it.

Thomas raised his brows. "My son is Joe Smith. He goes by Pointer."

Steen went still, looking sharply at the man. "Pointer?" He remembered Pointer all too well. The kid had walked into prison skinny and pale, the perfect bait for abuse on his first day. "He's your kid?"

At Thomas's nod, Steen relaxed. Pointer was a good

kid, and Steen had known instantly that the younger man came from solid stock. Maybe Pointer wasn't exactly a kid. He was in his early twenties, but his cushy life had left him too young and inexperienced to face prison on his own. He'd been targeted from the first second he'd stepped in the door, and it was Steen who had met his gaze in that first second. It was Steen who'd seen the fear in the kid's eyes, as well as the rigid set to his jaw that hid his terror behind a mask of defiance.

He'd liked the kid instantly. Pointer reminded him of how he used to be, back when he believed that if you fought for what you believed in, you could make it happen. He hadn't wanted Pointer to lose that look within the first five seconds of being in prison.

Thomas gestured toward Steen's left side, which was heavily bandaged beneath his shirt. The knife blade had gone deep, causing injury that his body hadn't wanted to heal, resulting in a rough second surgery. "I want to thank you for saving his life," Thomas said.

"Oh..." That. Steen didn't want accolades. He didn't deserve any. He shrugged. "Right place at the right time. Nothing else."

Thomas laughed softly, the kind of amused laugh that called Steen on his bullshit. "Pointer said you'd say that, but he knows damned well that he wouldn't have survived his first day in prison if you hadn't seen that knife coming for him and stepped in front of the blade to take the hit instead of him. He was targeted because of my work, and I'll never forget that you're the reason I still have a son." He leaned forward, looking at Steen. "I've seen the tapes, Steen. I watched your eyes go to that knife, and I saw you decide to step in front of the blade and take the hit that was meant for my son, who you didn't even know. I know how badly you were hurt, and I know you almost died."

Steen shifted uncomfortably, not used to that kind of praise. "Yeah, well, it worked out okay." He realized there was no point in denying it. The kid had seen the move, and apparently, the damn cameras had immortalized it. Maybe it was good that Pointer knew he'd been saved. Maybe it would encourage him to pay it forward to someone else someday. "Pointer's a good kid," he said, trying to get the focus off him. He was too damn tired to be lauded as a hero. He'd just done what any decent human being would have done. Nothing special. Just basic shit.

"I know he is, and now, thanks to you, he has a chance to start over." Thomas slipped his hand inside his blazer and withdrew a fat envelope. He held it out to Steen. "Here's some cash to help you get started. It's tough to get going after you've been in prison. It's my thank you for saving my son's life. I'm deeply sorry that you almost died because of it. I will owe you a debt for the rest of my life."

Steen stared at the envelope for a moment, but he felt no temptation to take it. He shook his head. "Money ruins people," he said. "I don't want it."

Thomas must have heard the conviction in his voice, because he lowered the envelope without trying to push the money on him. "What can I offer you?"

"Nothing." The only thing Steen wanted was to turn back the clock to four years ago, and have him be smart enough to see what was coming before it happened. But there was no way to make that happen. Life had happened, and there was no way to go backwards.

Thomas raised his perfectly trimmed eyebrows. "I know a lot of people, Mr. Stockton. I can make phone calls. I can get you a job doing anything you want. I can help you start over. I have money, and I have contacts in every line of business."

Mr. Stockton? Steen almost laughed. Who called him Mr. Stockton? "Just call me Steen." But he had to admit he was mildly curious as to what Pointer's father did for a profession. Who had a business that resulted in so many connections and favors? Maybe he was trouble after all. "Why did your business get Pointer targeted?"

Thomas's face became shuttered. "I piss off a lot of people," he said simply. "I accept those consequences for myself, but seeing Pointer affected has caused me to think deeply about what I do. Please, allow me to do something in return for my son's life."

Steen shook his head. "I don't want anything." He started to walk past him, then turned around. "No, you can do something for me."

Thomas raised his eyebrows. "Anything."

"Be the father Pointer deserves."

Thomas frowned. "That's it?"

"That's everything. You seem like a good guy. He's lucky to have you. Be there for him. Put him first. That's it." Steen suddenly felt restless, and he wanted to leave. "Have a nice day." He nodded his farewell, and then walked past him, heading down the driveway toward the chain link fences that separated the world from those who weren't allowed to inhabit it.

Today, they would open for him. He still remembered the day he'd arrived in the van, watching those gates slide shut behind him, locking him away from the world.

Thomas didn't follow as Steen walked away, his legs growing heavier with each step. He hadn't realized how weak he still was, but there was no way he'd go back to the infirmary and ask them to call a transport to take him to a civilian hospital, like they'd originally planned. He'd rather die under the oak tree by the street than have anyone tell him what to do ever again.

He'd made it only about a hundred yards when the gates slid open, and a black pickup truck towing a two-horse trailer drove in the gate.

Steen stopped, a slow grin spreading on his face as he watched it roll up. He didn't need to see the *Stockton Ranch* lettering on the side to know it belonged to his brother, Chase, the only person who would be disrespectful enough to pick him up when he'd specifically told him not to.

The truck eased to a stop beside him, and Chase rolled down the passenger window. His beige cowboy hat was tipped back on his head, and those familiar blue eyes regarded him unflinchingly. Chase draped his wrist loosely over the steering wheel, turning just enough to face Steen. "Need a ride, little brother?"

"I don't know." Steen walked over to the window and leaned on the frame, his elbows resting on the door. "Where you going?"

"Stockton Ranch. We have room."

For a moment, Steen hesitated. How many times had Chase talked about getting him to the ranch? It wasn't his world, and he didn't feel like he was a Stockton like the others were. "You don't want an ex-con living at your place. It's bad for business."

Chase's smile disappeared, replaced by a dark scowl. "I'll say this one time, Steen, and then this topic is over. We both know damned well that you didn't do shit, and you didn't deserve prison. The fact that justice failed you doesn't change the fact you're a good man, an innocent man, and my brother. The ranch will always be a better place with you on it. Got it?"

Unexpectedly, Steen's throat tightened, and he had to look away. "You never give up, do you?" But there was no ire in his voice. Just weariness.

"No, I don't. You coming to the ranch or what?"

Steen took a deep breath, fighting off his gut instincts to climb into the truck and accept the life his brother offered. He wanted it, he burned for it, but it wasn't right. Despite Chase's words, he knew he was a black mark on the Stockton name, and he didn't warrant a piece of that land. He wanted to just walk away and forget who he was, but he couldn't make himself do it...not yet. There was something he needed to know, closure he needed to attain before he could walk away. "Is Mira there? At the ranch? I have some questions to ask her."

Chase grinned, his entire face lighting up at the mention of his woman. "Of course she is. She lives there now. We've been waiting for you to get out before we get married. She said you promised to come to the wedding, and she's holding you to it."

Steen considered that statement. Marriage carried nothing but bitterness for him. "You trust her?"

"Yeah, all the way."

He heard the conviction in Chase's voice, which surprised him. Chase had been more anti-marriage than any of them. "Then I hope you're right. You deserve a good one."

"I got one." There was a thud from the trailer, and the sound of hooves crashing into the metal. Chase swore, glancing back at the shuddering trailer. "White Knight doesn't like the trailer. You want to ride with him?"

Steen stiffened. It had been a long time since he'd done the horse thing. "Not really."

The horse crashed against the side of the trailer, making it shake. A panicked squeal split the air, and Steen instinctively called out to the animal and began heading toward the trailer.

He'd never been able to walk away from a horse in need, and the old instincts came rushing back.

"Hey!" Chase called out.

Steen glanced back at him, still moving toward the horse. "What?"

"You'll need this." As he spoke, Chase tossed a battered old cowboy hat out the window. Steen recognized it immediately as the one he'd worn back in high school.

He caught it, surprised by the sensation of feeling that familiar shape in his hands again. "You still have this?"

Chase grinned. "I never gave up hope, bro."

Shit. It had been a long time. Steen studied the hat for a moment as images of his old life, his cowboy life, flashed through his mind. He remembered the horses, the competitions, the smell of worn leather and clean straw, all the things that had grounded him when nothing else had made sense. He felt like it had been in another lifetime, as if it had happened to someone else.

White Knight slammed against the side of the trailer again, jerking his attention back to the present. Steen jammed the hat down on his head and loped back to the trailer. He opened the door and swung inside without even thinking about what he was doing, moving as naturally as if he'd never walked away.

A dapple-gray horse was backed up against the rear of the trailer, his head up and his eyes wide with fright as the trailer began to lurch forward again. Steen instinctively began to talk, the words leaving his mouth without him even thinking of what to say. He just knew what the horse needed to hear, as he always had. The horse began to lower his head toward Steen, his ears flicking forward to listen, and suddenly, the day didn't feel so crappy.

For the first time in a long, long time, Steen felt like he was in the right place.

It wasn't much, and he knew it wouldn't last, but for right now, it was a start. He grinned at the animal. "Hey, boy. Sucks to be locked up in a cage, doesn't it?"

White Knight lowered his head even further, and he pushed against Steen's chest. Pain shot through his side, but he ignored it. Instead, he placed his hand on White Knight's nose, surprised by how soft it was. He'd forgotten what it felt like to touch a horse. He'd forgotten what soft was.

He'd forgotten a lot.

He just wished he'd forget the rest.

Chapter 2

Despite her valiant efforts to maintain a positive attitude, there was simply no way for Erin Chambers to see the bright side of the situation when the SUV she was driving lurched and slithered to an engine-coughing death on the edge of the Wyoming dirt road.

"Oh, come on. Please don't do this to me." She tried the ignition again, but there was no response from the vehicle that her best friend, Josie Mayers, had named "Faith" because the truck had gotten her out of so many sticky situations.

Well, Faith had bottomed out in a big way, and was so not living up to her name.

Erin grimaced as she flexed her hands around the steering wheel, trying not to freak out and collapse in a wail of self-pity at this latest sabotage to her attempts to make this day work out okay. She glanced at her watch, her heart sinking when she saw what time it was. It was almost six. It had been over an hour since she'd received the frantic call to stitch up a horse that'd had a trailer mishap.

As tempting as it was to surrender to Faith's refusal to move, she needed to get to the ranch, not sit by the side of the road awaiting the first Wyoming sunset she'd seen in over a decade.

Six weeks ago, it had sounded like a fantastic idea to use her upcoming sabbatical to run the Wyoming vet clinic so Josie could go to Chicago and help her mom recover from surgery. Erin had happily envisioned snuggly dogs, soft kittens, and long conversations with devoted pet owners, a situation that seemed so much more appealing than her stressful equine surgery practice in Virginia. She'd been excited to use her training to help animals that weren't under deep anesthesia all the time, and the thought of returning to the area she grew up in had sounded wonderful. She'd been struggling so much in her day-to-day life, and she was excited to reconnect with a life that used to make sense to her, hoping that maybe she'd be able to figure herself out in the process.

Today was her first day on the job. As she'd expected, she'd gotten conscious animals and the opportunity to drive around her old town, but other than that, it hadn't been anything like she'd hoped and expected, not by a long shot.

In the last twelve hours, she'd been knocked down and nearly impaled on the horn of a massive bull. She'd also been flattened into a mud puddle by a six-year-old girl practicing her barrel racing skills on whatever happened to be near her and her pony, which, at that time, had been Erin.

Her last stop had gone long when the sheep had escaped from the holding pen just before she'd arrived, necessitating almost an hour of watching sheepdogs do their stuff, which was incredibly cool, she had to admit, but not very helpful with her timing. She'd spent over two hours cumulatively being lost, since the spotty cell service in the region had rendered her reliance on her phone's GPS a poor decision. None of the landscape looked familiar to her, and she felt like a complete stranger in the land that had once been her home.

Except *this* life hadn't been her home. When she'd been a kid, she'd never been canvassing dirt roads, trying to locate assorted ranches. She'd been cloistered in the library, or at school, or at ballet class, or any of the proper training classes that her parents had thrust upon her. Everything about her return was wrong, nothing was as she'd imagined, and there was nothing she could do about it now.

Josie was gone, there was no one else to run the clinic, the engine was dead, and a horse named Ox's Ass needed stitches. A passing glance at her phone confirmed she had no reception, so there would be no white knight galloping to respond to a call for help. Grimly, she yanked open the glove box and pulled out the tattered spiral notebook that Josie had stashed inside as a makeshift owner's manual. She flipped the first page, quickly scanning Josie's notes. On the second page, she found a note stating: "When the engine dies while driving, there are three possible causes." Erin scanned the rest of the page, and her heart sank.

"Really? She wants me to connect wires in the engine? Seriously?" Josie's instructions seemed incredibly complicated, and Erin felt like tossing the notebook aside, crawling into the backseat, and sleeping until the three weeks were up.

But there was a horse with a torn shoulder, and she was the one who had to fix it. She sighed. Just because her parents were disgusted with her utter lack of mechanical ability didn't mean she couldn't manage to follow a few instructions, right? She pulled out her reading glasses and studied the notebook again. Sadly, and not surprisingly, the fact she could actually see the words clearly didn't make them any easier to understand.

No problem. She was an innovator. She could make this happen. She took a deep breath to fortify herself, and then popped the hood. Once she saw the engine, she was sure she'd be able to decipher Josie's notes. It was all good.

She pulled the door handle to get out...but the door didn't budge. "Oh, come on!" She twisted in her seat and then slammed her boot against the door. It opened with a reluctant creak of protest. See? She totally rocked it.

Trying not to think about the fact that feeling so triumphant over her ability to exit a truck maybe didn't bode well, she climbed out, her hiking boots kicking up dust balls in the roadside dirt. Ignoring the aches in her body, she strode around to the front of the vehicle, propped the hood up, and studied the engine.

Then she looked at Josie's drawings.

Then she looked at the engine again.

Then she looked at Josie's instructions.

Then she tried turning the notebook upside down.

"Seriously?" Was the drawing even of the same vehicle? Tears suddenly burned in her eyes, tears that had nothing to do with an engine, and everything to do with the fact that she'd been pressing on as hard as she could for the last twelve months since everything had fallen to pieces around her, and this stubborn engine was just one thing too much.

She gripped the grill of the truck and closed her eyes, willing herself to pull it together. She was not going to fail at this. Josie needed her, and Ox's Ass needed her.

Erin took a deep breath, and opened her eyes. "You can do this. It's not like Josie's a mechanic, right? If she can figure it out, then you can." She shook out her shoulders, then set the notebook on the engine. She stared at it. She willed it to make sense to her. But not one damned thing on Josie's drawing matched what she could see in the engine.

Dammit. She was not going to let Ox's Ass down, but what was she going to do?

Hike.

That was what she was going to do.

It was only a few miles, right?

She'd be there in two hours.

God, a two-hour hike carrying medical equipment? Really?

Yes, a two-hour hike carrying medical equipment. Really.

She was *not* going to let herself mourn for her sterile operating room and pristine working conditions. She'd left because that life was strangling her, and if it took hiking several miles in the dusk to find herself again, then that was what she was going to do.

Resolutely, she tossed the notebook on the engine and left it there, then marched around toward the back of the SUV. She'd just managed to get the stubborn tailgate open, when she heard the rumble of an engine.

She spun around, shielding her eyes against the sunset as a billow of dust filled the sky. A black truck pulling a horse trailer was heading right toward her. For a split second, she considered all the big city warnings about strangers and isolated roads, and then she decided that if she were kidnapped and held for ransom, it might help her to gain perspective on her own life. And, if she weren't kidnapped but got help instead, then that would be good, too. So, a win either way, no matter what quality of individual was in the truck.

Decision made, she stepped out into the road and began waving her arms to flag the driver down.

❀ ❀ ❀

Steen was in the middle of a deep conversation with White Knight about the crappiness of prison life and how much it sucked to have personal freedom ripped out of one's life, when he felt Chase slow down and stop the truck. Frowning, Steen glanced toward the window, knowing they hadn't gone far enough to reach the ranch, but there were no stop signs on these roads. When the truck stayed still, Steen raised the flaps on the side of the trailer and peered out, but all he could see were fields. Where were they?

He heard Chase's door slam shut as his brother shouted a greeting to someone. Apprehension flooded Steen, and he closed the flaps. The last thing he wanted to do was socialize. He had nothing to say to the world. He'd had nothing to say when he lived in it, and he had nothing to say now that he'd been removed from it for the last four years. How did a man make small talk when he had a prison record haunting him?

There was no chance he was getting out of the trailer.

He patted the horse's nose and resumed their conversation, keeping his whispers low so no one would know he was in the back. Knight was relaxed now, munching happily on the hay net that was dangling from the wall. His ears kept flicking toward Steen, listening to the conversation with more interest than anyone had shown in a long time.

Steen sat down on a hay bale, leaned back against the wall, and folded his arms over his chest as he stretched out his legs. His black motorcycle boots didn't fit with this environment, but it was what he'd been wearing the day he went to prison. He wondered idly if Chase had kept his old cowboy boots, in addition to his hat. Not that he'd wear them. His horse days were long past. Everything was long past. He had no idea what he was supposed to do now. Everything he'd believed in was history.

He pulled his hat down over his forehead and closed his eyes. He'd spent four years waiting, and he had no problem with waiting some more while Chase socialized. He was in no rush to go anywhere.

As he sat there, however, the sound of a woman's voice drifted through the window. The moment he heard it, something inside Steen went utterly still. He held his breath, straining to hear her better, *needing* to hear her.

Knight snorted, and Steen instinctively put his hand on the horse's nose, willing him to be quiet. Everything inside him was screaming to hear more. Who was she? Something thundered through him, and he knew he'd heard her voice before.

He stood up and edged over to the side of the trailer, leaning his shoulder against the metal wall as he strained to hear the conversation. He couldn't decipher the words, but her voice rolled through him, melodic and beautiful. He felt the tension in his muscles ease, as if he'd found somewhere safe for the first time in years. Who was she?

Memories hammered at the edges of his mind, moments of his life from long ago. A face flashed in his mind, the image of a thin, homely girl with thick glasses, braces, fancy clothes, and a smile that could light up a room on the rare occasions when something made her grin.

Erin Chambers.

Steen grinned, remembering the girl who had been three years behind him in school, so young and innocent that she'd been more like a fragile china cup than an actual girl. She'd been a nerd and a brainiac, from a family with more money than the rest of the town had, collectively. They were the kind of family which had disdained kids like him who were from the wrong kind of family, and the wrong kind of life.

But not Erin.

Erin was different. Erin had never wanted anything from anyone. She wasn't the type of person he'd ever bothered to notice back in those days, and it had been sheer dumb luck that had brought her into his sphere of awareness. He'd never forget the day he'd first noticed her—

The door to the trailer swung open, and Steen jumped back as Chase stuck his head in the trailer. "You still know engines?"

"Engines? Yeah." He'd spent a lot of time in the mechanics' shop in prison, and he'd even fixed the guards' vehicles in exchange for a break from harassment. "Why?" He was still reeling from the thought of skinny Erin Chambers. How was she still in the area? He'd been so sure she'd be some high-ranking corporate exec on the East Coast by now.

"A car needs your help." Chase gestured him out. "I'll stay with Knight."

Steen instantly comprehended the situation. It was *Erin* who needed his help. Erin, who had once looked at him like he was a saint put on the earth to save the world. She was the only truly selfless human being he'd ever met in his life, the only one who'd ever looked at him as if she couldn't see all the worthlessness about him. Yeah, she'd been nothing but a kid, and he'd never exchanged more than a couple sentences with her, but in some ways, she had been one of the most pivotal parts of his high school existence. A part of him wanted to go out and see her, to find out what she'd become, but a deeper, stronger instinct kept him rooted.

There was no chance in hell he wanted Erin Chambers to see what he'd become. She'd known him as a star athlete, the first Stockton to break from the rut of cowboy-life. He'd been big time, on the way to a full ride at the college of his choice, fully prepared to make a career far away from the small, cursed life he'd been labeled with. Then had come his career-ending knee injury during his junior year of college, right in the middle of an ass-kicking season that had everyone short-listing him as a top draft pick destined for a Hall of Fame career. In one split second, every one of his dreams had come crashing to a stunned halt.

And that's when the real descent had begun, a series of events outside his control that had derailed him from everything that mattered and every dream he'd ever had.

Chase gestured again. "Come on. She's in a hurry."

"No."

Chase tipped back his hat. "No? Really?" It wasn't a question. It was a challenge, the kind that Steen never used to back down from.

This time, however, he didn't respond to the bait. "No," he repeated, even more firmly.

His brother's eyes narrowed. "I don't care if you've been

in prison for four years. The only thing that separates us from our father is the fact that, despite everything, we value human beings. If you sit in there and refuse to help, then you're no better than he ever was."

Anger ripped through Steen. "I'm not him."

"You've got his genes. We all do. It's up to you to fight them. The first time he went to prison, it turned his soul black for good. You want to be him? You want to go there?"

Steen scowled at his brother. "You're a bastard."

"So are you." Chase stepped back, looking down the road. "Erin," he yelled out. "My brother's coming to help you. He's just got to get his pants on first."

He heard Erin yell something back, and Steen glared at his brother, who was now grinning broadly. "You're an ass."

Chase tipped his head. "Why, thank you. I appreciate the compliment."

Steen knew he had no choice now. He'd been busted. He gave Knight a final pat, then ducked out the door and stepped into the sunlight. Squinting against the brightness, he took a deep breath, and then turned toward the front of the truck, steeling himself for the sight of a skinny, intellectual rich kid who had moved far beyond his station in life.

What he saw was a woman in hiking boots and muddy jeans, with a thick ponytail cascading down her back as she leaned over the engine of a beat-up Chevy. The setting sun was igniting auburn streaks in her hair, making it look like fire was sizzling through the strands. Her hair was mesmerizing, the most insanely beautiful thing he could remember noticing in his life. The skinniness was long gone, replaced with the kind of womanly curves that he could spend hours memorizing. Her light blue tee shirt was muddy and torn at the hem, and she was muttering under her breath, talking to herself about something.

He grinned, remembering all those times he'd seen her talking to herself as she'd wandered through the school. Erin Chambers indeed.

At that moment, she looked up at him. The moment her brown eyes fastened on him, he felt like his entire world had gone still. She wasn't the skinny geek he remembered. She was a woman who literally took his breath away.

It was Steen Stockton.

Erin couldn't believe the man standing before her. After all her years of fantasizing about him, wondering what had happened to him, searching the web for information about his football career after he'd blown out his knee in college, he was standing right in front of her.

An old, faded cowboy hat was pulled low over his forehead, almost shielding his dark eyes from her view. His face was clean-shaven, his jaw angular and defined. He was wearing a black tee shirt, black jeans, and boots that would fit more with a motorcycle helmet than a cowboy hat. His shoulders were still wide and his body angled down to a V toward his narrow hips, but he was lean, too lean, and his cheeks were sunken, as if he'd been in a bad place for a long time. He was all male, well over six feet tall, and his muscles were hard and cut beneath his shirt, despite his leanness.

He was no longer a boy, but the man she'd envisioned. He was raw heat, with a languid grace that she knew hid his lightning quick reflexes and innate physical grace. For the first time in years, she felt a pulse of physical attraction. Involuntarily, her gaze flicked to his mouth. His lips were pressed together, as if he were trying to contain the words that wanted to escape. Sexy and silent, just as he'd always been, only now, he was so much more.

In the face of the sheer strength of his presence, she suddenly felt like the ugly, geeky fourteen-year-old again, hopelessly outclassed by the only person she'd ever known who lived life on his terms and didn't care one bit what anyone else thought of him.

He frowned. "You okay?"

Erin suddenly realized she'd been gaping at him. Horrified, she snapped her mouth shut, trying to regain some semblance of self-respect. "Yes, fine. Thanks. It's so incredible to see—"

"You need some help with your engine?" he interrupted, cutting off her sentence before she could finish commenting on how good it was to see him.

It was her turn to frown now. Did he not recognize her? After all these years of fantasizing about him whenever she'd needed to escape from the reality of her life and marriage, he didn't even *remember* her?

Desolation flooded her, the kind of utter loss that happens only when a dream is shattered, a dream that had all its power because it was pure fantasy, and therefore could never be destroyed. And yet, in one instant, he'd shattered it, because *he* was reality now, standing in front of her. Steen had been the only one who'd ever looked *at* her, instead of *through* her, but it apparently hadn't meant anything to him, at least not enough for him to remember her.

She lifted her chin resolutely. It didn't matter. She knew her imagination had elevated him into the perfect man. Even though the real life man didn't even *remember* her, it didn't change the fact that he'd been her salvation and her escape throughout the years. She knew he was a good guy, and it wasn't his fault that she'd been such an insignificant blip in his life that he didn't remember her.

He tipped his cowboy hat back, giving her a clear view of his eyes for the first time. They were haunted. Deeply haunted. She was shocked by the change in them from the jaunty, arrogant boy she'd known in high school. There was no humor in his gaze. No life, even. Just emptiness. Her heart tightened, and instinctively, she reached out, touching his arm. "What happened to you, Steen?"

She'd never have believed anything could take him down, but something had, something that had broken the spirit of the man she'd believed in for so long, the one who had lived in her heart for over a decade.

Chapter 3

Steen froze, and his muscles went rigid under her touch, making her realize that she'd overstepped her boundaries in a major way. She quickly jerked her hand back. "Sorry, I didn't mean to—"

"You recognize me?" he asked.

She blinked. "What? Of course I do. How could I not?" Did that mean he recognized her? She wanted to ask, but she didn't dare. His gaze was too intense, and his silence was too unyielding.

After a few moments, she began to shift uncomfortably. She cleared her throat, and tried to change the subject to one that wasn't quite so incredibly awkward. "So, um, you know engines? Is that right?"

"Yeah." He still didn't take his gaze off her face, which she found both completely intimidating and wildly intoxicating. She used to catch him watching her when they were in school, but his face had always been inscrutable and distant. Now, however, there was so much intensity burning in his eyes that her heart started to race. No longer were his eyes empty and apathetic. They were simmering with heat, and all of it was directed at her.

So much for the fantasies not living up to reality. Even in her dreams, he'd never made her feel the way he was making her feel in this moment, like she was the only thing in his world that had ever mattered. Flustered, she pulled her gaze off him. "Well, um, here." She grabbed Josie's notebook from the engine. "I have this diagram of what I'm supposed to do if Faith dies, but

I can't figure it out."

"Faith?" He still didn't take his eyes off her, not even to look at the notebook that she was waving at him.

"My car. Josie's car. Do you remember Josie? She was my only friend...I mean, she was my best friend in high school. Anyway, she's a vet out here, but she had to go to Chicago to help her mom through surgery, so I'm out here for a few weeks taking over her clinic while she's gone. So it's her car, and I don't know how to use it and—" She stopped when the corner of his mouth tipped up in a slight smile. "Sorry. I'm babbling."

"You used to be so quiet," he said. "I think you spoke more words just now than you uttered during your entire high school career."

"I used to be so quiet?" She stared at him as the meaning of his words sunk in. He remembered her from high school? The liar! *He remembered her!* Elation flooded her, and she couldn't stop the silly grin. "I'm still quiet," she said. "That was just a momentary babble because I'm nervous. So, don't get used to it. I'm not suddenly going to become a talker."

His right eyebrow quirked. "You're nervous? Why?" As he spoke, he plucked the forgotten notebook out of her hand and walked around her toward the engine.

"Because you make me nervous."

He glanced over at her as he leaned over the engine. "Me? Why?" There was an edge to his voice that was like steel.

"You always have." She leaned against the side of the truck and folded her arms over her chest, watching him as he looked back and forth between the notebook and the engine.

He tossed the notebook over his shoulder and braced his hands on the truck, his gaze methodically scanning every inch of the engine. "Why?" He repeated the question, not even bothering with polite preamble. He wasn't even looking at her, but she felt his intense awareness of her.

"Because you're you."

"That's not an answer." He bent over and fiddled with something in the shadowy recesses of the engine.

Her heart began to pound as silence built between them. She knew he was waiting for her answer, and a part of her wanted to give him the absolute truth. She'd never see him again after she left in three weeks, right? After so many years of suppressing every emotion and trying to be the woman who everyone in her life wanted her to be, now was her chance to speak up, to admit who she was, to let it all out. To take a chance. That's why she'd come out to Wyoming, right? Because she'd been dying inside, and she'd been desperate to find some kind of kick in the pants that would get her heart beating once again.

He twisted something and moved a wire, still waiting for her answer.

After a moment, he looked up. "She's all set," he said, his voice rumbling through her. His gaze was boring into her. "You're good to go." He waited a heartbeat, and she knew this was her last chance. In a split second, he was going to lower the hood, and she was going to drive away.

She swallowed and lifted her chin. "You made me nervous in high school because I had a huge crush on you," she said, speaking a little more quickly than she intended. When his eyebrows shot upward in surprise, she hurried onward, not wanting to hear him disdain her confession. "You always looked at me like you saw I was there. No one else did that. I mean, I was the new kid, only there for high school while my dad was starting up a new surgical unit at the hospital. I couldn't believe the captain of the football, basketball, and baseball teams noticed *me*. For a fourteen-year-old girl to be noticed by someone like you…well, it's huge. I always thought that you'd figure out I wasn't worth acknowledging, that someday you'd stop *seeing* me, that I was going to do something that would get me kicked off your radar." She couldn't read his expression at all, but he was watching her intently. "So, yeah, that's why."

He stood up, slammed the hood shut, and then leaned on it, still watching her. "And now? Why do I make you nervous *now*?" Again, that edge to his voice that made her want to both step away and also to reach out to him and take away whatever had caused it.

She swallowed and shrugged. "It's still the same."

Her words hung out there between them, silence mounting.

"You're not fourteen," he finally said. "It's not the same. It's completely different now." His gaze swept over her breasts in a swift, almost unconscious move that made her heart start to race. He'd noticed she was a woman. Dear heaven, *he'd noticed she was a woman.* When she was in high school, even though he'd noticed her, there'd never been anything romantic or sexual in the way he'd looked at her. But now? That last look from him had been searing hot.

"No," she agreed slowly, trying to keep her voice even. "I'm not fourteen. That's different, and that's why I'm nervous." When she was thirteen and he'd been a junior, he'd been untouchable, a crush that was safe because their worlds kept them too separated. When she'd been fourteen and he'd been a senior, they'd both been in high school, but the gap between them had been still be insurmountable. But now? The three years between their ages made no difference, and they both knew it. Not that she was going to say it. She'd said as much as she was brave enough to say. She was so far from bold, so not the kind of person who claimed what she wanted. She was actually really impressed she'd said that much.

Steen levered himself off the truck and walked around the grill, coming to a stop inches from her. She stiffened, trapped between the truck and his body. His gaze roamed her face, never, to her dismay, dipping below her chin, before it settled on her eyes again. "I'm not the kind of guy any girl...or woman... should have a crush on. I'm not one of the good ones."

Outrage rushed through her. In high school, he never would have said anything like that. He'd thought he owned the world back then. "What happened to you, Steen?" Again, she reached out instinctively.

When her hand landed on his upper arm, he didn't tense, and he didn't pull away.

He went still, but this time, she was pretty sure he leaned into her touch ever so slightly, as if his soul wanted it but his mind refused to accept it.

Time seemed to stand utterly still, and then he carefully lifted her hand off his arm. Her heart started to pound as he cradled her hand in both of his, his touch warm and soft, despite the strength of his hands.

"You always looked at me like I was a prince," he said, his voice rough. "And you're looking at me that same way right now."

She felt heat rise in her cheeks. "I don't—"

"No." He shook his head. "Don't apologize. It's incredible. I never want you to look at me any other way. It needs to stay that way. I need it to stay that way." He raised her hand to his mouth, and pressed a kiss to the back of her hand. "I'll freeze the expression on your face right now for the rest of my life, so that it's imprinted in my mind forever. Thank you for that. I wish you every last bit of good luck and good fortune with your life, wherever it takes you when you leave here."

For a moment, she forgot to breathe, stunned by the feel of his kiss. He smiled faintly, a smile of lost time and old memories, as he brushed his fingers over her cheek. Then, abruptly, he dropped his hand, turned, and walked back to the trailer and out of her life.

Again.

※ ※ ※

Steen leaned back against the chimney of the bunkhouse, clasping his hands behind his head as he watched the sun set over the hills. The roof was cool and hard, and it felt good, just uncomfortable enough to remind him he was alive.

So…Erin Chambers was a vet. He smiled, a deep sense of satisfaction pulsing through him. He'd always figured she'd succumb to her potential and run a billion dollar company somewhere. It had pissed him off to think of her selling out, and now he didn't have to have that on his list of things to hate about the world anymore. Erin had somehow stayed true to herself and had become a vet.

Damn.

Seeing her today had made things feel right in his world, even if it was just for a minute. His smile faded as he thought of the way she'd looked. Those jeans had fit her like pure sin, and the mud on her shirt had been sexy as hell. Her eyes had been vulnerable and honest when she'd watched him. Shit. He could still feel the heat from her gaze as she'd stared at him, the hunger in her eyes so obvious that it had taken all his willpower not to slide his finger along her jaw and take her mouth with his. She was all female, awakening every possessive and predatory male instinct he owned. He'd never reacted so strongly to a woman as he had today.

He'd wanted to pin her against that rusted truck with his body and sink his hips against hers. He'd burned to feel the softness of her body against his, to feel the curve of her hips beneath his palms. He'd wanted nothing more than to angle his head and kiss her. Not just a kiss. He'd wanted to breathe her soul into his, and wrap his entire being around hers, protecting her from how shitty the world really was.

He'd always felt protective of her, but today? Today had been about her as a woman, and him as a man. It had been pure desire, the kind of need that wound up with nakedness and endless nights of loving. He grinned, clasping his hands behind his head as he stretched his legs out on the shingled roof and thought about Erin. For four years in prison, he'd never had a moment like this. A moment of simply being still, without looking over his shoulder, thinking about something that made him smile.

Hell, there hadn't been anything to think about that would make him smile.

Not that he cared about the void that had been his life for so long.

It had been worth it to wait for this moment. He hadn't been lying when he said he'd remember the expression on her face for the rest of his life. He wasn't a prince, and he wasn't a good guy, but hell, to have Erin looking at him as if he was…it made him feel like maybe there was a chance there was something good left inside him.

He looked out across the ranch, his vantage point giving him a good view across the acreage. A few horses were grazing in a distant field, beside a massive rock he remembered sitting on as a kid, when he'd gotten pissed at Chase for dragging him out here to work on the ranch. He'd used the rock as a place to go when he was mad, but the truth was, he'd liked being on that rock. He liked being where no one could lay a hand on him or get in his face. Like now. On this roof, no one was in his space, and he hadn't had that for a long time. Four long years, to be exact.

"Steen?" A voice that felt distantly familiar caught his attention.

He looked down to see a woman standing in the dirt outside the bunk house, her belly sticking out so far it looked like she'd shoved a bowling ball under her shirt. She was wearing black leggings and sneakers, as if she were about to head off to a yoga class, not traipse around a ranch dodging dung. "Yeah?"

"I'm Mira Cabot, Chase's fiancée. He asked me to come out and tell you dinner's ready, if you want to come up to the main house and eat with us."

He sat up abruptly, studying her. So, this was Mira Cabot, the woman who had dragged him back from the edge of death? He didn't recognize her at all…except her voice. It seemed to settle around him like something soft and warm, and he knew he'd heard her talking to him that day in the hospital. He'd been consumed by the urgent need to find her and ask her what she'd said, but now that he could see her, he wasn't sure he wanted to. She looked like a normal person, not some soothsayer who had gifted him with some deep wisdom. He'd waited so long to ask her…and now…something in his gut knew that whatever she had to say wasn't going to live up to what was in his mind. So he shrugged casually, dismissing her invitation to dinner. "Thanks, but I'm all set. I don't need anything."

"Really?" She set her hands on her hips, glaring at him. "You're way too thin, your face is pale, and your cheeks are sunken. You look suspiciously like someone who almost died from a stab wound not too long ago, who bailed from the hospital before he was supposed to. Correct me if I'm wrong, but it seems to me that eating is a basic requirement to healing."

He stared at her, dread leaping through him at her comment. How much did she know? Yeah, he'd been in the prison hospital for a while, and then back in his cell, but recovery was slow in prison, especially since he'd been in bad shape before the injury, surgery, and then the complications had knocked him further on his ass. But before the panic could set in, he realized that she couldn't know his secrets. She was just being herself, irreverent and irritating…and perfectly her. He grinned, despite his crankiness. "You talk to Chase like that?"

"Only when he's pulling some manly crap that warrants

it." She grinned back, her face creasing into a genuinely warm and welcoming smile. "Get down here, Steen. I didn't give you my best advice on your deathbed just to have you rot away out here on your roof."

Steen's smile vanished at her reference to their deathbed chat, which stirred up his curiosity again. He decided that maybe he did want to know. "Hang on a sec." He carefully inched down the roof, and then swung himself to the ground, successfully managing not to flinch or grimace at the stab of pain in his side. He landed beside her, surprised by how short she was. She'd seemed bigger when she was giving him attitude. "I have a question for you."

A question that had been gnawing at him for months. It was time to get it answered. He needed to know.

Chapter 4

She smiled. "Of course." She tucked her arm through his. "You can ask me as we walk to the ranch house."

Steen grimaced. "I'm really not feeling social—"

"No problem." She began to propel him toward the house. "You can be sullen and quiet the whole time, but as long as you eat, it's all good. Chase made some sort of beef stew he said was your favorite, so you better eat it."

Steen glanced toward the house that had once belonged to Old Skip Johnson, who'd owned the ranch when they were kids. Steen had been invited inside the main house only once, unlike Chase, who'd been buddies with the old man. Chase had really made him Old Skip's beef stew? He loved that shit. Guilt hammered through him. He knew Chase was reaching out, but he just couldn't meet his brother halfway. He didn't know how to bridge the gap he'd erected between him and his brother. "I'm not staying long," he said. "I won't be in your way."

"Not staying long?" Mira stopped and put her hands on her hips. "You have to stay. Who's going to watch the ranch while we're gone?"

"Watch the ranch?" Suspicion flared in Steen's mind. "What are you talking about?"

"I need to go back home to get the rest of my belongings and sort through my parents' stuff. I can't fly now." She patted her big belly. "So we're taking a road trip. Chase said you'd run the ranch while we're gone."

Steen narrowed his eyes and glanced at the house again.

"I haven't been around horses since I was sixteen—"

Mira laughed, a laugh that was so genuine he almost felt confused. Who had a reason to be that happy? "I wasn't a horse person either, but I took care of things when Chase ran off to call you back from the dead." She poked his chest. "I think the least you can do is run the ranch for your brother. He was really worried about you, you know." Her brow furrowed. "He loves you, Steen. You know that, don't you?"

Hell, she was talking about love to him? He didn't want to have this kind of conversation. "Fine, I'll eat," he said gruffly, hoping that would get her to lighten up. He started stalking toward the front door, then gritted his teeth when Mira tucked her hands around his arm again, like they were best friends.

He didn't have best friends, and it made him feel trapped the way she was holding his arm. He didn't know how to respond to it, so he did nothing. He just walked, trying to focus on not accidentally bumping into her whenever the pain made him list to the side.

"What did you want to ask me?" she asked.

He glanced at her. She looked so happy, and so sweet. He was cynical as hell when it came to women, but there was something about Mira that he liked, and even trusted. He could see why she'd won Chase over.

She smiled encouragingly. "Chase is going to come out on the porch in a couple seconds, so ask me now if you want it to be private."

"Yeah, okay." He tipped his hat back and rubbed his forehead as he stopped. "So, yeah, when I was unconscious, Chase said he brought you to talk to me." He didn't want to say that he sort of remembered her being there. That felt too corny. He'd been dancing with death when she'd shown up, and everyone knew it. How could he possibly have heard what she said to him? But he had. He just couldn't remember what it was, but he knew it was important.

She nodded. "Yes. He thought I might be able to reach you. They were afraid you'd given up trying to live."

He didn't answer her unspoken question, knowing full well that she was right. That was exactly what he'd done. He'd used the injury as an excuse to pack it in, but his brothers had

had other ideas.

She peered at him. "It's okay if you did give up for a bit, you know. Sometimes it's hard to keep going when you don't see hope."

"Yeah, well, sure." He cleared his throat, and then rubbed the back of his neck restlessly. He so wasn't used to these kinds of discussions, and he'd rather shove a pitchfork in his foot than talk personal with anyone, let alone a woman, but he couldn't walk away until he got his answer. "What did you say to me? Chase said you were the one who brought me back. What'd you say?"

She smiled, her eyes softening. "I told you that there was a woman out there who was waiting for you, someone who needed you, someone who only you could save. If you died, you'd leave her alone."

He was startled by her answer. She'd called him back by waxing on about a *woman*? "Really?"

She nodded. "Really."

That wasn't what he'd expected at all, on any level. Women had betrayed him so many times, so deeply, that the last thing he would ever do is stay alive for one. "Are you sure? Was there anything else?" This couldn't be what had been driving him to survive. It was impossible.

Mira's dark brows went up. "Of course I'm sure. I was there, and I was definitely paying attention to the words coming out of my mouth." She sighed. "I know that the men in your family have issues when it comes to women. I thought your brothers were going to shoot me when I told you to keep on living because a woman needed you. They all thought I was going to drive you over the edge." She beamed at him. "They were wrong."

He shook his head, feeling even crankier. "I'm not like my brothers." Although he'd come to live in the Stockton hellhole for good when he was twelve, he'd never felt that much of a bond with the other boys who'd lived in that shack and shared his last name. His mother had never been married to their dad. She'd been knocked up and gone on with life, dropping him off occasionally when she needed childcare. When he was twelve, she'd finally told him she couldn't deal with caring for him, so she was turning him over to his dad, an alcoholic bastard who took his rage out on his sons, who all bore the scars of his abuse. Steen had gotten lucky, because he hadn't moved in until later. The problem was that moving in so late in life, he'd never developed the same bond with the others. He didn't belong with them then, and he didn't belong with them now. He certainly didn't warrant a free handout of a hundred acres.

Mira was watching him, an expectant look on her face, as if she were waiting for him to tell her what woman he'd come back to life to rescue.

"Well, I appreciate your help," he said, somehow managing to be polite. There was something about Mira that made him want to be nicer than he actually was.

He was feeling strangely desolate after her answer. He'd been building so much into her answer, hoping that it would somehow shed light into the darkness that had no exit. Instead, she'd talked of women? "I'm done with women, though."

"Obviously not, since that's what woke you up." She tapped his chest, right over his heart. "You were meant to survive for a reason. Don't run away from it."

His head began to ache, and his side started throbbing. After years of never having any space to himself, all he wanted was to be alone. Away from people, away from conversation, away from those who thought they knew what was right for him. He was done with this, with all of it. "I'm going back to the bunk house. I'm beat. Long day."

"A long four years, more like," she said.

"Yeah, that too." He was restless and antsy, and he wanted nothing less than to go into that ranch house and sit around a table with Chase and his pregnant fiancée, like they were some happy little family. "Tell Chase I'm sorry I missed dinner." He was just turning to head back to the bunkhouse when the screen door opened and Chase walked out.

"You got him out here." Chase's cowboy boots clunked on the deck as he walked over to them. He'd cleaned up, and was wearing dark blue jeans and a collared shirt, like a respectable cowboy. He walked up to Mira and draped his arm over her shoulder to pull her against him. She beamed up at him, and he grinned at her, a moment of intimacy that made Steen look away.

He couldn't do this. He couldn't be around them. This was so not his world. "Listen," he said, risking a quick glance at his brother. "Can I borrow some car keys? I'm going to go into town."

Chase frowned. "I made dinner."

"Yeah, I know." Steen shook his head. "I need some space. I need to look around. Maybe get a job." Doing what? Pumping gas? Because that was what he'd been doing when the shit had gone down. Pumping gas. No, he wasn't doing that again. There was no way he was going back to that life. There had to be something more. Something else. But what? He felt like he was drowning.

Chase shook his head. "No way, man. This is your first night home. Dinner's on me. It's real food, bro. You've forgotten how good it tastes."

Steen thought of the thick stew that he used to love. He could still smell the rich aroma of it simmering, that mouthwatering smell of fresh baked bread for dipping... "Bread, too?"

"Yep. You in?"

Steen shrugged, his stomach rumbling despite his reluctance. How good would a home-cooked meal taste? Even if Chase totally messed it up, it would still be damn good. It had been forever.

"And you can't get a job," Chase added. "We need you on the ranch while Mira and I—"

"I know. Road trip." Steen glanced longingly down the long, dirt driveway. He wanted so badly to get on his old bike and drive, just drive until the world didn't exist. "Can't one of the other guys do it?" They had brothers. A lot of them. Too many. All of them who were closer with Chase than he was.

Chase shook his head. "They have other stuff." He set his hand on Steen's shoulder. "I need to do this for Mira, Steen," he said, his voice low. "She needs to go back, and I want to be there for her. Help me out. This place is yours as much as mine, if you ever want it. There's ten acres on the south side that's yours. It's got a great site for a house."

"Live here?" Resistance flooded Steen. "This isn't my

world."

"It could be."

Steen met his brother's gaze, and shook his head once. He didn't want to make a scene in front of Mira, and he didn't want to be an ungrateful shit. "I appreciate it," he said finally. "I appreciate that you and Mira and the others pulled me back from the edge." Well, he wasn't so sure he appreciated that, to be honest. "I appreciate that you tried, and I'm sorry you got sucked into my crap."

"Yeah, you should be. You owe me." Chase grinned, looking entirely too happy. "The only way to pay me back is to eat my dinner, and then watch the ranch. If you still want to leave when I get back, I'll give you your old bike and you can go. Deal?"

Steen jerked his gaze to his brother. "You have my bike?"

"Yeah, I salvaged it for you." He held up a cell phone. "I also have one of these for you. It's not charity. It's necessary while you're managing the ranch, so don't argue."

Steen ignored the phone. "Where's my bike?" His fingers curled, as if he could feel the handlebars beneath his fingers.

But Chase shook his head and waggled the phone at him. "Dinner and ranch-sitting first."

Shit. He had no money to buy another one, and Chase knew it. His brother had him by the balls. He glanced down at Mira, who was watching him with a soft expression. He was surprised by the look in her eyes. She wasn't judging him, despite the fact he was being an ungrateful sod to the man she was going to marry.

Suddenly, he felt like a shit. Just because he'd failed at his life didn't mean Chase and Mira had to suffer. He took a breath, and managed a smile. He didn't want to be the guy everyone thought he was anymore. He had a chance to start over, and he wanted to take it. Dinner and ranch sitting for the brother who had saved his life seemed like a decent step in the right direction. With a scowl, he grabbed the phone out of his brother's hand and shoved it in his back pocket. "Yeah, okay. Dinner and I'll watch the ranch, but I'm not moving into your house."

Chase laughed and slammed his hand down on Steen's shoulder. "I'm almost a married man, buddy. I'm not going to complain about having you sleeping far enough away to give me a little privacy with my woman. The bunk house is all yours."

Mira's cheeks flamed red, and she poked Chase in the chest, much like she'd done with Steen. "You're such a pig, Chase. You're sleeping on the couch tonight just for that remark." She rolled her eyes at both men, and then marched inside. Steen thought he heard her giggle just before the door slammed.

Chase grinned as he pulled the door open and held it for Steen. "She never makes me sleep on the couch," he said with a wink. "But I like earning my way back into the bed."

"Shit, man." Steen grimaced. "I don't need to hear about stuff like that." Women? Dating? Romance? Stuff like that made his stomach turn, and all his alarms start ringing.

He'd learned his lesson, and he'd learned it well.

He might be willing to sit through dinner with his brother, and he could be coerced into watching over the ranch, but women? That was one road that had burned him badly enough that he was never going down it again. Ever. It didn't matter what Mira had said to him. It really didn't.

But as he followed his brother into the kitchen, Erin's face flashed through his mind. Had there been pain in her eyes when she'd looked at him? Was she the one who needed to be saved? Because if it was her…well…she was different.

Shit. He couldn't do that. Not even for Erin. *Not even for her.*

Chapter 5

Five days later, Steen was pretty sure he'd made a colossal mistake in agreeing to watch over the ranch while his brother was gone. Chase and Mira had been gone less than two days, and Steen was convinced the job was going to kill him. He'd already gone the "almost dead" route, and now that he'd reclaimed his place in the land of the living, he wasn't sure he was ready to go down that road again. He wasn't ruling it out indefinitely, just not at the moment, and he really didn't want to die shoveling horse manure.

He set down the hay bale and leaned over, bracing his gloved hands on the hay as he tried to steady himself. His mind was spinning, and his back was drenched with sweat from the effort of fighting off the pain in his side. When had he become such a lame ass that he couldn't do basic physical labor? Yeah, true, he'd been feeling a lot stronger this morning than he had a few days ago, but he'd pushed it too hard and now he was paying for it. He hadn't even done that much. Shit. He was pathetic.

He bowed his head, struggling to catch his breath. A few minutes of rest, and he'd be fine. Just a minute—

"Hello? Is anyone here?"

Steen jerked upright the moment he heard Erin's voice echo through the stables. He moved so fast that everything spun, and he had to grip the wall of the stable to keep from staggering. Swearing, he closed his eyes and wiped the sweat off his brow, hoping that Erin would just disappear and not walk down his aisle—

"Steen! What's wrong with you?"

He swore and turned to face Erin as she jogged down the aisle toward him. Her dark hair was in a loose ponytail, with the wavy ends pulled forward over her shoulder. Her jeans fit her just right, and her muddy tee shirt was much too snug over her breasts for his comfort. What did him in, however, was the look of concern on her face. She looked so damn worried about him that he felt the tension in his chest ease, and he was able to stand taller.

"Nothing. I'm fine." He made himself release the bars, and was pleased to discover he was perfectly capable of maintaining his balance unassisted. Score one for a quick recovery. "What's up? Why are you here?" The moment he asked the question, he winced. He sounded rude and obnoxious, which he generally was, but he didn't want to be that way with Erin. "I mean, yeah, good to see you again."

A small smile curved the corner of her mouth as she stopped in front of him. "Is it now? Delightful, in fact? Is that what you were trying to say?"

He watched the way the sunlight from the open barn door made the auburn highlights glisten in her hair. "Yeah, kinda. Delightful sort of works." Delightful wasn't a word he'd ever used in his life, but it seemed to fit the moment. He kind of liked it, actually. Delightful. *Delightful.* Erin the Delightful. Erin with hair that looked delightfully tempting, like it was begging for him to run his fingers through it. Yeah, delightful worked in a whole lot of ways when it came to Erin.

Her smile became wary, and she put her hands on her hips. "So, I'm here because Josie had the ranch on her schedule for a deworming treatment today. All the horses."

"All of them?" Steen dragged his attention from her hair and refocused on her face. He noticed that there were circles under her eyes, and she looked tired. He narrowed his eyes. "Late night?"

"What?" She frowned. "No, of course not. Do you have the horses ready?"

He glanced down the aisle at the empty stalls. "Not so much." There were at least thirty horses on the grounds right now, more if he counted the two small herds that were roaming the high plains. Almost all of them were turned out in the assorted fields on the ranch at the moment.

"Not so much?" She looked around, as if noticing the silence of the aisle for the first time. She sighed, giving him the kind of impatient look that made him want to grin. "Josie's notes said that Chase always brings them in so I'd be able to go right through them."

"Yeah, well, you didn't get Chase today. You got me." Steen tipped back his hat and wiped his forearm over his brow. "He's out of town for a few days, and he didn't mention it. I didn't see that on the schedule. We'll have to reschedule." A part of him wanted to ask her to stay until he could round them up, just so that he could be around her, but he wasn't that much of a fool. The longer she stayed, the more of him she'd see, and the less of himself he'd be able to hide from her. "See ya."

He turned away and gripped the hay bale, but when he lifted it, the pain was so great that he had to set it down again. Shit. He'd totally pushed it too hard today. He leaned on the bale, trying to catch his breath, grimacing when he heard Erin striding along toward him.

He didn't look up, hoping she'd get the point, but instead, she crouched down next to the hay bale and peered up at him, her brown eyes steady. "Guess what, Steen."

Damn, she smelled good. What was that smell? Lavender? It was so faint he almost couldn't catch it. Not perfume. Maybe just the soap she'd used in her shower. "What?"

"Did you know vets go to medical school? Did you know that we can tell when someone is in extreme physical distress? It's a handy talent sometimes, you know?"

He narrowed his eyes, and gave up the pretense. He eased down to his knees and braced his forearms on the hay, taking the strain off his body. "I'm recovering from an injury. I just need a sec. I tweaked something."

"An injury?" Her eyebrows went up, and he was annoyed to discover that he thought she was even sexier when she was looking stubborn and mutinous. The hero-worship thing she'd had going on in high school had had its own appeal, but her "don't mess with me" attitude was awesome. "And what would that injury be?" she asked dryly.

A stab wound in prison that nearly killed me, a surgery that saved my life but left a mile long scar down my body, and then a second surgery to clean up the shit from the first time around. The truth sounded so crappy he'd never say it aloud, not to her. So, he shrugged. "I got cut."

Her gaze flicked to his right side, where his most recent incision was, her intuition apparently not failing her at all. "I want to look at it."

His entire body went molten at the idea of her hands on his skin. "I don't think that's a good idea."

"Why not? Because my image of your manly prowess will be shattered when I see that you actually bleed like everyone else?" She made her way over to his left side and knelt beside him.

"No," he gritted out. "Because I'm afraid you won't be able to contain yourself when you see my incredible physique. You know, since you have such a crush on me and everything. I'm not in a dating mode right now, so I'd have to turn you down, and it could get awkward." Total lie. There was no chance he'd turn her down. It was the opposite problem entirely.

She laughed, breaking his tension. "I'll take my chances, hot stuff. I'll do my best to refrain from throwing myself at your feet and begging you to rip my clothes off and do lots of naughty things to me."

Naughty things? His imagination surged into overdrive as a dozen naughty ideas raced through his mind. Suddenly, his side didn't hurt anymore. All his blood had gone straight south, and was accumulating way too fast for a guy of his discipline.

She tugged lightly at his shirt. "You want me to disrobe you, or do you prefer to manage these things yourself?"

He looked over at her, trying to think about baseball and not the erection that he was starting to get. "Can't you go away?" Yeah, he was being completely rude, but he couldn't help it. He needed to get rid of her now, before she started seeing things about him that he didn't want her to know.

She grinned, entirely undaunted by his surliness, which, if he'd had to guess, he should have predicted. She'd never seemed intimidated by him, even when she was a gangly fourteen-year-old and he was being an arrogant jerk with his friends. That was one of the reasons he'd always been fascinated by her. He sensed that she saw right through his bullshit, which was intriguing as a general rule, but right now, it was decidedly inconvenient.

She patted his shoulder. "You're a worse patient than the Rottweiler I had this morning. Now shut up and be good, or I'll have to muzzle you."

"Vet humor," he muttered, barely hiding his grin. He was too cranky to laugh, but damned if she didn't make him want to do it anyway. With a melodramatic grimace, he dragged his shirt out of his jeans and pulled it up. He knew there were bandages on it, so she wouldn't be able to see that it was a knife wound.

She leaned forward, apparently inspecting his side. She said nothing, and he was just starting to relax, when he felt her hand on his side. He was so surprised by the touch that he jumped sideways.

"It's okay," she said softly. "I won't hurt you. I'm just looking."

Her voice was soft and gentle, just like she probably used on her animals, but it worked. He felt the tension ease from his body, and he went still, his entire being focused on the next touch. This time, when her palm flattened against his side, he was ready for it. He couldn't believe how warm her skin was, or how soft. He closed his eyes, drinking in her touch, absorbing every nuance of what it felt like. He couldn't remember the last time he'd felt anything so surreal, and so perfect. He bowed his head, his gloved hands digging into the prickly hay, tracking the movement of her fingers down his shoulder blade, along the bandage, and along his waist.

She spread her palm against his ribs, as if she were trying to hold his heart inside his body. It felt good…no, amazing… no, incredible.

"Steen?"

"Yeah." He wanted to tell her not to stop, but he had no words. The sensations had gone way beyond naughty things and disrobing. Her touch was searing deep into his soul, making parts of him respond that had nothing to do with his cock.

"The bandage is pretty soiled. You're bleeding through it. The skin around it isn't hot yet, so I don't think it's infected, but it's going to be if you don't get it cleaned." She moved her hand along the edge of the bandage again, a gentle touch that somehow seemed to strip the tension from his body. "You need to go to the doctor and have it checked."

"You do it." The words were out of his mouth before he'd even thought them, but the moment he said it, he knew it was what he wanted. "No doctor." He couldn't go back inside closed walls again, not yet. A hospital was like a prison, with locks on the doors and doctors who told you what should be done with your body. They'd ask him questions, and then it would go in his file that he was an ex-con with a stab wound. He didn't want to go there. He didn't want to be that guy, not anymore, not again. "You," he said again.

"Me?" She dropped her hand from his side. "I'm a vet."

He looked over at her. "Please."

She met his gaze, and he saw something in her eyes soften. Somehow, she'd understood the depth of his need without him having to explain it. "Okay, but don't complain if you wind up with fur and a tail by the time I'm finished."

Relief rushed over him. "Deal. Do you have time to do it now?"

"I have all afternoon, since we're not deworming." She stood up. "Wait right here. I'll get some supplies from Faith. Whatever you did to her worked. She's been rocking along perfectly."

"No problem." He stood up as she rose to her feet. She was less than a foot from him, and suddenly the air between them became heated and thick. Silence fell, and he felt that same urge overcome him, the need to touch her, taste her, and drink her into his soul.

Slowly, he pulled off one of his gloves and brushed his fingers over a loose tendril of hair that had escaped from her ponytail. He expected her to pull away, but she didn't. She sucked in her breath, but didn't retreat.

He rubbed the strands between his fingers. "So soft," he said. "I always wondered."

"You did?"

"Yeah." He met her gaze. "But now, it's a different kind of curiosity."

She swallowed. "Because I'm not fourteen."

"Because neither of us are teenagers." He opened his hand and slid all his fingers through her ponytail, watching the strands slide over his skin. He couldn't believe how soft it was, and he was mesmerized by the sensation of the strands against his skin. "I forgot that things this perfect existed."

"No. Don't say that," she protested, her body suddenly tensing. "I'm not perfect. I'm so tired of trying to be. Please, of anyone in the world to say that, don't let it be you."

The edge to her voice caught his attention, and his gaze moved from her hair to her eyes. This time, for the first time, he saw pain he hadn't seen before. Not physical pain. The kind of pain that etched itself deep in one's soul and never went away. He knew that kind of pain, because he lived with it every day. The realization that she carried that same kind of burden made his fingers curl more tightly in her hair. Suddenly, she wasn't the brilliant, rich girl who would always outclass him. She was a woman who carried the same burdens that he did. She was the same as he was, which made her reachable, touchable, and accessible.

His fingers tightened in her hair, and he tugged gently, needing more. "Is there a Mr. Erin back home waiting for you?"

Again, a flash of pain, but she shook her head. "Just me."

There were a thousand more questions he wanted to ask, and a thousand reasons to walk away, but he did neither of those things. Instead, he stripped off his other glove, and then did what he wanted to do most of all: he took her face in his hands and kissed her.

Chapter 6

Erin's heart hammered in her chest the moment she realized Steen was about to kiss her. Dear God, after all these years? It was really going to happen? She started to panic, but his fingers tightened in her hair, drawing her closer to him as he bent his head, trapping her.

His grip was so warm and gentle that all her fear fled, and she lifted her face to his. He closed the distance between them, and he kissed her, a true, perfect, real kiss that was so much more than anything she'd ever imagined. The moment his lips touched hers, all the years of fantasy dissipated, and all that was left was the reality of who he was, of this moment, and the feel of his lips on hers.

His mouth was decadently soft as he lightly kissed her, a touch so gentle that she was almost afraid she'd imagined it. It was beautiful and sensual, a caress so tender it belied the tough, arrogant attitude he worked so hard to convey. How could this rough cowboy possibly deliver a kiss so sensual and beautiful that it made her heart come alive? But he did.

Steen paused, his lips hovering over hers, as if giving them both the chance to back away.

She didn't retreat, and neither did he. Time hung in suspended animation as she waited, her entire soul yearning for more. Would he kiss her again? Or had this moment been all there would be? For a split second, she considered pulling away, not wanting to be the one who was rejected, but before she could do so, he kissed her again, his lips feathering over hers in the softest of kisses, like a butterfly that had just spread its wings for the first time.

He kissed one corner of her mouth.

And then the other.

It was the sweetest, purest, most innocent kiss of her life. It made her feel treasured and respected, as if she were an angel held in the palm of her guardian, protected against every negative moment in the world. It wasn't the kiss of a man who saw her only as breasts and a way to get off. It was the kiss of her knight, her salvation, a man who had declared himself her savior through one simple kiss.

Hope leapt through her as Steen kissed her again, hope that there was still beauty left in her, hope that there was still something magical in her world. Instinctively, she reached out and wrapped her fingers in the rough cotton of his shirt. She needed to touch him, to ground herself in his strength, to hold him close.

He pulled back slightly, not far, but enough that she could see into his eyes when she opened hers. His dark eyes searched hers, as if he was looking for the answers in her soul. Then he smiled as he lightly brushed her hair back from her forehead. "Erin Chambers," he said softly, his voice almost reverent.

It sounded so amazing to hear him say her name, and she smiled. "Yes?"

"You need to say no." His eyes darkened, and his expression became more intense. "You need to let go of my shirt, step back, and tell me that I'm not good enough for you. You need to do it right now, or I'm going to think I deserve this, and I'm going to kiss you again."

Her heart ached at his words, at the loss of arrogance he'd once carried with such pride. "I want you to kiss me again," she whispered. "I don't want to let you go."

He took a deep breath that mingled with a groan, then his hands came to her cheeks, his palms cradling her face as if she were a fragile crystal that could shatter at any moment. "Don't say that," he said. "I can't do this to you."

"Do what?" Kiss her? Make her feel like she mattered? Treat her like she was the most precious treasure he'd ever encountered?

"Drag you into my world." He traced his thumbs over her cheeks, a touch so soft and tender it made her entire soul burn for more. "It's such a bad place, where I live," he said, his voice low and rough. "I don't want you in it, and I don't want you to see it."

She knew he wasn't talking about his house, and her heart bled a little bit for whatever tragic lessons life had taught him since she'd last seen him. "I don't care." She tugged on his shirt to drag him closer, stood on her tiptoes, and then kissed him.

For a brief moment, one that felt like an eternity, he didn't respond at all. Embarrassment flooded her. Had she completely misread his reluctance? Had he actually *meant* it when he'd said he didn't want to kiss her again? Horrified, she started to pull back, but before she could retreat, he palmed the back of her head, cutting off her retreat, and then he kissed her the way she'd always dreamed of.

It wasn't chaste and sweet this time. There was nothing pure or innocent about it. This time, his kiss was searing passion and insatiable want, poured into an erotic temptation of tongues, lips, and need. His mouth tasted like sinful seduction, and his kiss was demanding and deep. He plunged past all her inhibitions and defenses, coaxing her into a tangle of tongues so intense she felt every nerve ending in her body ignite.

She released his shirt and slipped her arms around his neck. The moment her hands were no longer between them as a barrier, Steen wrapped his arms around her and hauled her against him. His torso was rock hard against her, a tower of strength and heat. Her breasts were tight against his chest, and her nipples became hard instantly, almost aching with need. He locked one arm around her waist, and his other hand slid beneath her shirt over her lower back. He traced her spine upwards, and then palmed her back between her shoulder blades, pressing her even more tightly against him.

The feel of his hand on her bare skin was incredible. Hot, rough, and demanding. His fingers kept catching on her bra, and she found herself desperate for him to find the clasp and unfasten it. She wanted his hands on her breasts, and his mouth on her nipples. She wanted every part of this incredible man to become hers. With him, maybe she could be the woman she'd never managed to be, the woman who was sexy enough to keep her man's interest—

Sudden memories flashed through her mind, dozens of incidents of embarrassment and failure, as a woman and as a lover. What would Steen do when he realized what she was really like? How fast would he run? Oh, God, no. She couldn't do that. She couldn't live through a rejection by Steen. She could handle being dismissed by anyone except him, because he was the light that had kept her going all these years.

Tears filled her eyes, and she pulled back, stepping out of his embrace. "I can't do this."

"What?" He stared at her, his eyes so dark and turbulent that she wanted to throw herself back in his arms and pretend she wasn't who she was. "What's wrong?"

"Nothing. I just—" She tucked her hair behind her ear, wishing she could be any place but in that barn with Steen. What had she been thinking by kissing him? Fantasies were better left as fantasies. She could never deliver on the intensity of what was sizzling between them. "I just remembered another appointment. That's all."

"Another appointment?" His eyes darkened, and he walked over to her, closing the distance she'd just managed to put between them. He caught her chin lightly between his thumb and forefinger, forcing her to look at him. "Don't lie to me, Erin. I can take it from anyone else, but not from you."

She saw the plea in his eyes, and the confusion, and her heart seemed to shatter. "I'm sorry," she whispered. "I'm just a mess. I just got out of a really terrible marriage, and I...I haven't been kissed in a really long time, let alone done anything more. It's just...I know you're..." She bit her lip, wanting to hit him for not looking away and giving her space. "God, Steen! You've been with so many women, and you're this great expert, and I just... I'm just extremely insecure when it comes to sex, and especially with you." She rolled her eyes and pulled away. "God, how could I even go there with you?" She started to walk away, then spun back to face him. "You've been my source of hope and strength for all these years. In my fantasies, I'm good enough for you.

I don't want that shredded by reality. I couldn't take it if you rejected me, too." She gestured back and forth between them, trying to articulate what she was feeling for him. "This thing between us is amazing. I'm shocked that you've been thinking of me all this time, like how I've been thinking of you, but don't you get it? If we tried to make it real, then it disappears. We both lose what little hope it gave us."

He sighed, and ran his hand through his hair. "Erin, you've got it so wrong—"

"No, I don't." She held up her hand. "I don't want to talk about this anymore. Kissing you was amazing and incredible, but we're going to leave it like that, okay? I'm going to go get my supplies and fix your bandage, and then I'm going to leave, okay? Okay. Great. Fine." She flung up her hands and stalked out, not waiting for his response.

She didn't want him to call her back…but she did. She wanted more than anything for him to fight for her, to announce that he believed in her, to declare that he'd waited so long for this moment that nothing would hold him back from being with her, no matter how pathetic she was.

But he didn't say that.

He didn't say a word.

He simply let her walk away.

And her heart, which she hadn't thought could bleed anymore, crumbled into its last pieces.

᪥ ᪥ ᪥

Steen braced his hands on the stall door, his mind reeling as he replayed Erin's comments. He didn't even know which one to react to first. He was furious that she'd been married to someone who made her feel like shit. What kind of bastard did that to a woman, let alone to *Erin*? She was an incredible woman, and he couldn't imagine how she'd been treated to make herself believe otherwise. What had she endured?

Then…oh, man, he couldn't believe her comments that she wasn't good enough for him. Was she insane? She'd always been so far out of his reach it had been laughable, but now he was an ex-con with a rap sheet? Yeah, he was even lower on the totem pole now. She should *never* feel less than the amazing woman she was. *Ever.*

But she did. Clearly, she did.

She was such a wreck that she'd come out to Wyoming to try to recover. She was halfway through her trip, and she was clearly no closer to getting her self-confidence back. Was he really going to let her walk away like that? Or was he going to do something about it?

He was going to do something about it.

"Okay, are you ready?" Her voice was brisk and business-like as she walked into the barn, carrying some sort of hard, plastic case. Her chin was up defensively, and she had pulled a baggy sweatshirt over her tight tee shirt.

He ground his jaw in irritation at the distance she was trying to put between them. He'd tried to stay away from her, but it was different now that he understood her situation. She needed him. He'd never been in a position to help anyone before, and he liked being that guy for her. He *wanted* to be that guy for her. Maybe Mira was right. Maybe Erin was the reason he was still alive…because he was supposed to help her.

Granted, he wasn't going to lie: he had liked kissing her. A lot. More than a lot. It had been the best kiss of his whole cursed life, and he wanted more because he simply couldn't get enough of her. But more than that, he wanted to be the guy to rebuild her.

Steen wasn't worth a lot, but he knew that one thing he could do would be to show Erin how incredible she was. He saw every amazing detail about who she was, and if she saw herself the way he saw her, she'd never again take shit from a guy who didn't honor her.

"Can you lift your shirt?" she said impatiently. "I'd like to get this done."

He studied her for a long moment, ideas swirling in his mind as he studied her. "How long are you in town?"

"Ten more days." She gestured at his shirt. "Can you lift it up, please?"

Ten days? He had less than two weeks until she was gone from his life. His gaze swept over her again, this time appraisingly. He noted again the circles under her eyes, the pain etched in her face. Could he take that away in such a short time? Make her realize how amazing she was, so she could go back to her life and claim it the way she deserved? For ten days, he could keep her from seeing who he really was and what he'd become. He could make it about her, and give her the gift that she'd always given him: hope of a better place in life, hope of being more than he thought he was.

"Steen?" She waved a hand in front of his face. "Are we doing this, or not?"

He grinned at her, unable to suppress the surge of anticipation. "Oh, yes," he said. "We are definitely doing it." And it was going to start right now.

He didn't bother to lift his shirt the way she'd instructed. Instead, he grabbed the bottom hem and dragged it over his head, so he was completely naked from the waist up.

Not surprisingly, Erin's eyes widened in a response so genuine and innocent that he wanted to laugh. This was going to be about her, for sure, but he was going to love every second of being with her. He was primed to reignite the fire that had once burned inside her. Yeah, he knew that helping her was going to require him to get in deeper than he wanted. When she left, she was going to take a piece of his soul with her, but at the same time, she'd leave behind something that would sustain him for the rest of his life.

He was in, and he was going to change her world, forever.

Chapter 7

Erin hadn't been ready for so much skin. She hadn't been remotely prepared for the sight of Steen's bare torso, rippling with muscle, and detailed with a stallion tattoo across his right pec. A long scar stretched across his abdomen, one that was somewhat recent, but definitely healed. It made him look even more dangerous, like a man who had survived hell and was still standing. He was pure male, and her stomach tightened instantly.

She wasn't used to responding to men. It had been so long since she'd been attracted to a man, but the awareness leaping through her was like fire igniting a part of her that had been hiding for a long time. When she'd walked in with her medical kit, she'd had lofty plans of focusing on his injury. She'd been so sure she'd be able to convince herself to remain detached, as if he were one of the horses she usually operated on.

She'd totally lied to herself. There was no chance she was going to be able to convince herself that the man in front her wasn't Steen Stockton. Not only was there no chance she was going to convince her subconscious that he was comparable to a horse, but she wasn't even going to be able to delude herself that he was simply a patient. He wasn't. Not to her.

He was Steen Stockton, in the living flesh. He was also half-naked, grinning at her as if he'd just figured out how to cause some serious trouble in her life.

Oy.

Men. More trouble than they were worth. But she

couldn't help the thrill of anticipation at the way he was looking at her.

In a last ditch attempt to protect herself from him, she gave him a good, solid glare before turning her attention to the bandage. She'd just managed to get it off when he interrupted her focus.

"How long were you married?"

She sighed. This was why unconscious horses were better patients than conscious men. "I don't really want to talk about that, thanks." She studied his side. The bleeding was from what was clearly a surgical incision, but next to it was another scar, a jagged, rough-looking one that looked about the same age as the one on his stomach: somewhat recent. Her eyes narrowed thoughtfully as she assessed it. "Is that scar from a knife wound?"

"Yeah. How long were you married?"

"Six years," she said absently, her attention focused on his injury. "How did you get cut? This looks like it was very serious. Given the placement of it, if it had gone deep enough—" Her gaze jerked to his face in sudden understanding of why he appeared so lean. "Did you almost *die* from this? Is that why you look so thin? Is that what the scar on your stomach is from? Surgery to save you?"

He tensed ever so slightly. His reaction was barely noticeable, except for the fact she was studying him so intently. "Maybe. Check the new incision. That's the problem now. They had to fix stuff up. Just let me know if it's good. What was his name? Your ex-husband's? Are you actually divorced? Was he a vet as well?"

She bit her lip, unable to stop herself from tensing at the thought of the man she'd trusted enough to marry. "Yes, we're divorced. It's been over a year. His name's Louis, and he's a heart surgeon. He pioneered a new procedure that will save the lives of many people."

She couldn't quite keep the irritation out of her voice. He'd been such a star on every level, which made his betrayal even worse. She bit her lip against the sudden tightness in her throat. Damn it. Why did she still let him get to her? Why couldn't she just get over it? Well, she could, and she would. That was why she was in Wyoming on a working vacation, right?

Because somewhere in the land of her messed-up childhood was the answer, or at least that was what she hoped. But first, more importantly, was Steen, a welcome distraction from the life she was trying to forget. "You almost died?" She set her hands on his, studying his face. "How on earth did you get cut badly enough to almost die?"

His gaze flickered toward hers, and she saw the evasiveness in his expression. "It's a long story. What did Louis do to you, Erin?"

"Nothing." She would not be a victim, and replaying her life just gave it power.

He cocked his eyebrow, and she knew he could tell she was lying. Guilt tumbled through her, and she sighed. Steen was right. She didn't want to lie to him. So, instead, she raised her eyebrows back at him. "Okay, so it wasn't nothing, but it's nothing I want to talk about." She would never forget that night, that moment, when everything had changed. Her hands started to tremble just thinking about it, so she shook out her hands, trying to keep her focus. "Why do you want to know so badly?"

"Because it helps me know how to get beneath those prickly spines you have up." He grinned. "I want to get under the spines, Erin."

She froze, her gaze snapping to his. "You do?"

At his slow nod, anticipation rolled through her. She suddenly felt a little warm. Yes, he was stubbornly ignoring her decision to keep a safe distance between them, but it was the most delicious sensation to have Steen pursuing her ruthlessly. It made her feel like there was something special about her, something that was worth going after.

Not that she was going to do anything with Steen, for a thousand reasons, most importantly because her soul was so fragile that she knew that even the slightest breeze would shatter it forever. She was holding on by the most delicate filament, and Steen had the power to sever that last hold she had on her ability to cope and be strong. "Don't."

He cocked an eyebrow. "Don't what?"

"You know what I'm talking about." When he continued to gaze at her intently, she flushed under his inspection. "Damn you." She cleared her throat, turned away, and began assembling her supplies to clean his still-healing incision, which was quite small and innocuous compared to his other scars. "I already told you that nothing is going to happen between us. No kissing or fondling of any nature. That means we don't need to have personal discussions about our past romantic lives, okay?"

"No, not okay. I'm not going to lie, I liked kissing you. A lot. I'm not ready to go away."

Despite her best efforts not to care, a little stab of excitement raced through her. She bit her lip, so frustrated she was responding to him. "I'm not ready for a relationship," she said quietly, almost not able to believe she was saying it. This was Steen, the man she hadn't stopped thinking about since he graduated high school and left town so long ago. How could she say no? Except she was. She had to. "Listen, Steen," she said as she began to clean the wound, "I'm too broken right now for anyone, including you."

He didn't flinch at her ministrations, but he turned his head to watch her. "I don't think so."

"But I know so." She said as she studied his assorted scars. She wanted to kiss away the pain she knew he must have endured. Her heart broke for what he'd suffered. Had there been anyone to sit by his side and tell him not to give up? She had a feeling he hadn't allowed anyone to come close, even if they'd wanted to. Was he like her? Keeping everyone at a distance? It was a terrible way to live, but she didn't know what else to do. "I came out here to heal and to find myself," she said as she laid the fresh bandage over his injury and rewrapped him. "I need space to be me." She finished and stepped back, needing desperately to retreat from the temptation he offered. "Looks great. You're all set. So, I'll see you around—"

He turned toward her and caught her wrist. "Who is the you that you're trying to find?" he asked, his dark eyes boring into hers with the same penetrating stare he'd always had. "Talk to me, Erin. I'm not a stranger."

A part of her wanted desperately to sit down and pour her heart out to him, to abandon the pretense of being the strong, amazing woman that she had always aspired to be. But at the same time, she couldn't afford to open the floodgates, or she was afraid she'd never be able to go back to her life and step back into the role she'd given everything to attain. Silently, she shook her head. "Steen, let it go. Please."

He frowned at her for a moment, still holding onto her wrist. Finally, he inclined his head ever so slightly. She wasn't sure if he was acknowledging her request, or if he was having a slight muscle spasm, because his stoic expression gave away nothing. "How about a trail ride?" he said. "I have to go check the herds at the far pastures."

She blinked. "Ride? Horses?" It had been so long since she'd ridden a horse. She operated on them almost every day, but her only focus was on them as patients who needed help, not them as animals that could be a part of regular life. "I'm not sure I remember how to ride. I've only done it a few times."

He grinned. "Me either. I haven't been on a horse since I was sixteen. You'll be my backup if I fall off and crack my head open on a rock." He raised his eyebrows. "You could take care of that, right?"

A little chuckle escaped at the image of Steen, who had once been one of the best calf ropers in the state, toppling off his horse and cracking his head open. "Yes, I could use prairie grass and saliva to tape you back together."

"Great. Let's do it. Yeah?"

She hesitated. The part of her that had spent her entire life working to prove herself and surpass the next hurdle recoiled from the idea of taking the afternoon off from work to simply enjoy herself. But another part of her, the broken part, cried for the chance to simply breathe, instead of frantically trying to accomplish one thing after another with no respite.

She felt like she was free-falling into an abyss, like a great black cloud was crushing her soul. She was desperate, and a little terrified that she couldn't seem to pull herself out of it. Maybe a horse ride was what she needed. Being out in nature, breathing in the fresh air, and feeling the wind on her face would give her clarity. She knew there had to be an answer as to how to reclaim herself, if she could just find it.

Steen grabbed his shirt and tugged it over his head. "I know you're free, because you had the rest of the day booked for this ranch. So, let's go. You need it. I can tell." He grinned, flashing her that old-school boyish grin that had made all the girls go weak. "Besides, this might be your only chance to see how hot my ass looks in chaps. It's worth it."

She burst out laughing then, a welcome relief from all the tension that had been building. "You have old-man saggy butt now," she retorted. "What woman wants to see that?"

"You do." He winked at her over his shoulder as he swaggered down the aisle, giving her a very good look at a rear end that looked every bit delicious as it had in high school. His jeans set low on his hips, owning his body with just the right amount of attitude.

She so should run for the hills, or at least try to get Faith to limp her way down the road and back to the clinic. But her feet wouldn't move. She didn't want to be the responsible, dignified Erin Chambers anymore. She wanted to be, for one day, the relaxed, devil-may-care woman who was daring enough to ride off into the sunset with a sexy cowboy who knew how to kiss.

Steen paused at the doorway to the tack room, looking back at her as he tipped his cowboy hat back, giving her a playful look that made her want to laugh. "You coming, Chambers?"

She grinned and made her decision. "Yes, I am. I definitely am."

Maybe it would be a mistake.

But maybe, just maybe, it would turn out to be the right choice.

She was tired of being afraid to try.

Fail or not, she was doing it. And as she closed her medical kit, she couldn't keep the grin off her face. Either way, it was going to be fun, and fun was something that she hadn't experienced in a long time...especially with a man who kissed like he was pure sin itself.

Chapter 8

By the time Steen led his horse outside to mount up, he realized that he'd been a stupid, lust-crazed idiot to suggest a ride with Erin. Not because heading off into the hills with her was a bad idea. Nope, he was still on board with that. But getting onto a horse? Shit. It had been completely natural for him to suggest a ride at the time. The implications hadn't even occurred to him… but they were now…

He wasn't sure he could do it.

Erin was already mounted, sitting comfortably on a mare named Winter Storm that he'd recalled Chase mentioning was mellow enough even for him. He, however, was holding the reins of a skinny, wild-eyed horse named Rock, which he'd noticed his first day. Rock was a little thin, a lot hostile, and plenty scarred up, making Steen pretty sure that Chase had rescued it from somewhere. Steen had always been interested in the horses that had come from messed up places, and he'd been having some good chats with the animal. When he'd decided to take Erin out on a ride, his instinct had been to head right to Rock's stall to give the horse a chance for a little freedom.

But now, as he eyed the skittish animal, he realized he should have remembered he wasn't the same person he'd been when he'd ridden the rebels. Back then, he'd been a reckless teenager with a body that could absorb any hit. Today, he was a man who knew exactly how far he could fall.

Rock's hooves were dug into the dirt, and he was eyeballing Steen as if he was going to test him every inch of the ride.

"What's wrong?" Erin asked, too damned perceptively.

"Nothing." For a brief moment, Steen contemplated calling off the ride, but when he glanced over at Erin and saw the excitement gleaming in her eyes, he knew he'd do whatever it took to keep that light fueled. He'd made a promise to help her heal, and he wasn't going to fail within the first ten minutes.

But as he put his foot in the stirrup, his back began to ache, the age-old ache that never left. Swearing, he jerked his boot out and leaned on the saddle, his hands braced on the leather as Rock swung his head around to watch him warily.

"Steen? Is it your side?"

He gritted his jaw. "No."

"What's wrong?"

Frustration roiled over him, anger that he'd set himself up for Erin to see him like this. "I broke my back a few years ago," he snapped out, unable to keep the edge out of his voice. The memories were too vivid, dredging up the fear that had almost destroyed him. "I'm not sure it's a good call for me to ride. Rock's a little skittish." There. He'd said it. What a fucking pansy he was.

But in truth, he'd never forget what it had felt like to wake up after his motocross accident. He'd been battered as hell, but the worst moment of his life had been when he'd tried to move his legs, and nothing had happened. For two hellacious weeks, he'd been paralyzed from the waist down, and his doctors had told him he needed to prepare himself for the reality that he might never walk again.

Jesus. That day...those weeks...the fear had been insurmountable. His entire life had been built around physical activities. Every moment that anyone had ever looked at him as if he was worth something had come from sports: calf-roping, football, baseball, and then, finally motocross, when football had no longer been an option after his knee had blown out.

He'd been absolutely devastated the day he'd shattered his knee and learned that he'd never play football again. His career had ended less than two days before the NFL draft, in which he'd been highly touted to be one of the top picks and destined for a legit career as a pro ball player. He'd given every last breath in his body to football, knowing it was his best chance to break the cycle of the life he'd been born into, and to lose that ticket had been *crushing*. That devastation, however, had been nothing compared to the moment when he'd thought he would be paralyzed for the rest of his life. He'd felt like his world had just ended, and it had been a brutal road back to get his body working again.

Yeah, in the end, he'd proved the doctors wrong. They'd been impressed as hell, and said he wasn't at risk of becoming paralyzed again, any more than anyone else. What did they know? They'd been wrong about his ability to recover, right? What if they were wrong about his vulnerability, and he took a chance that wound up with him in a wheelchair forever? They weren't the ones who'd have to live with it if they were wrong. He couldn't take that chance again. Ever since that accident, he'd been living on edge, so careful not to ever take that chance again.

It hadn't even occurred to him ten minutes ago that horses would put him at risk…until he'd put his foot in the stirrup and thought about how many times he'd fallen off over his life. Would the wrong kind of fall do him in? *Jesus.* He closed his eyes, and fought off the rush of fear.

Erin didn't give him a break. "But you have such a way with horses. Just talk to it like you used to do. He'll be on your side."

He looked over at her, surprised by her comment. "Talk to them? How do you know I used to talk to them?"

Her cheeks turned red, and she shrugged. "One time, I was out at the ranch helping the vet. You were in the corral with a wild pony that people were calling Psycho. Everyone was watching, so I came over. He was totally freaked out and panicking, until you walked over to him and started to talk. You didn't do anything else. You just stood there and talked. His head came down, his body relaxed, and he turned his head to listen to you. After a few minutes, he walked over to you and pressed his head to your chest. It was absolutely incredible. I've never seen anything like that in my life, and I've worked with a lot of horses. Everyone said you had a gift that day, and I saw it too. You remember that day?"

He was shocked by her story. Now that she mentioned it,

he did remember that horse. His real name had been something like Texas Hellion, but Psycho had been written on his halter when he'd shown up at the ranch, literally rescued from the proverbial glue factory by Old Skip, who felt it was his duty to rescue at least one hopeless, helpless horse per month. Psycho had gotten the golden ticket of a second chance that month, but by the time Steen had arrived, even Old Skip had given up on him. The trailer had been on its way to the ranch to take him away from his last hope…until Steen had connected with him. He'd saved that horse, and it had been the best damned feeling. He'd quit the horse scene a couple months after that, but he'd never forget Psycho.

Rock turned his head, studying Steen.

Steen studied him back, inspecting the animal's dark brown eyes. There was fear in there, but also curiosity, which was a good sign. As he and Rock inspected each other, he felt his own instincts taking over, rapidly assessing the animal, trying to ascertain what he would respond to.

"Talk to him," Erin suggested. "Do that thing you do."

"That thing I do?" He rolled his eyes at her vague, irreverent word choice to describe the depth of his connection with horses, but at the same time, her easygoing tone made him relax. He could talk to Rock. That was easy. It was what he did. He bent his head toward Rock's. The horse lowered his head, so that his cheek was pressed against Steen's. Steen grinned when he felt the horse's warm breath against his face. Shit, it had been a long time. "See, here's the thing, big guy," he said softly, too softly for Erin to hear. "I'm trying to impress a girl, but if I get paralyzed again, I'll be pissed as hell. I can't do that, buddy." Just the thought of it made a cold sweat break out across his brow.

Rock nudged his cheek, and blew on him again.

Sweat began to trickle down Steen's back, and he bent his head closer to the horse. "You with me?" he asked softly, using the same tone he'd used so many times before. "I need to know." He stared into the horse's eyes, and the animal didn't look away. There was a scar over his right eye, one that looked like it had taken a lot of stitches to heal. "You almost lose your eye, buddy?" Steen traced his fingers over the scar, and the horse's eyes closed slightly as he went still, letting Steen touch him.

Something inside Steen shifted, and he suddenly didn't want to be the guy who was grounded anymore. He didn't want to live in fear or regret, like he had for so long. He wanted to be in that saddle. He wanted to ride next to Erin and be the guy she needed for the next ten days. He wanted to be the man who saved her, and he wasn't going to do it living in terror of the shadows that had haunted him for so long.

He took a deep breath, shaking the tension out of his shoulders. "Okay, let's do this." He jammed his foot into the stirrup, grabbed the saddle, and then...paused.

Was he really going to do this?

He felt Erin watching him, and determination surged through him. Yeah, he was going to do this. What did he have to lose? If he got paralyzed, at least he'd know he'd fought to live instead of skulking in fear. He'd rather live for an hour with Erin by his side, than spend another thirty years existing in the half-life he'd inhabited for so long. So, yeah. He was doing this. With grim determination, he swung his leg over Rock's back, and settled into the saddle for the first time in years.

Rock tensed, and Steen instinctively leaned forward to stroke the animal's neck, talking under his breath. It took several minutes, but Rock's ribs finally expanded with a deep, shuddering sigh, and Steen knew that the trust had begun. He looked over at Erin, surprised to find himself wanting to grin. "Ready?"

She smiled back, her eyes so warm that something inside him slipped into place. He realized suddenly that she understood exactly how difficult it had been for him to get on that horse. She said nothing, giving him his privacy, but she *knew*. She always knew. She was the one person in the world who always saw through his shit to the real person beneath... and she was also the one who had always stood by him.

No wonder he'd been willing to risk paralysis for the chance to help her.

"You bet I'm ready," she said cheerfully. "Which way?"

Steen pointed toward the north cliffs as Rock shifted beneath him, dancing to the left with a few quick sidesteps. Steen instinctively moved with him, his body relaxed as he shifted his weight to keep himself perfectly balanced on the horse. So easy, so natural. He couldn't believe he'd been so afraid to try. "Lead the way, Doc."

Erin flashed him a grin, and swung Stormy's head toward the far pasture. She nudged the mare into a gentle lope, and Steen quickly caught up to her. It was surreal to feel the strength of the animal beneath him again, to be a part of such physical talent. He hadn't felt that kind of strength in a long time, not from himself or anything in his life. Riding the motocross bikes had been a rush, but that had involved a machine, not an athlete. With Rock, he could feel the flexing of muscles, the rush of adrenaline, and the sheer power that only a living being could create. God, he'd missed this. *He'd missed this.*

He took a deep breath, letting the clean air fill his lungs as Erin laughed with delight. "This is amazing," she called out to him. "I forgot what it was like to be riding instead of operating!"

"Want to go faster?" The thrill of the ride was building, that same rush that had galvanized him as a youth when he'd been calf roping, and then later when he'd tried the more socially and financially lucrative football field. He wanted to feel the wind on his face, and feel the power of the living creature beneath him.

"Yes!" She urged her horse onward, and the duo suddenly shot ahead. Stormy's neck stretched out as she lengthened her stride, and Steen grinned as Erin's laughter floated over the wind at him.

"Come on, boy," Steen said softly to his horse, gently urging him forward. After a moment of hesitation, Rock began to extend his legs, reaching farther and farther with each step, as if he, too, had forgotten what it felt like to be free. All hesitation dissipated as Steen and Rock raced across the fields. This was who he was. This was how life was supposed to be lived. It felt incredible, and he was suddenly so glad that he was out there. He never would have dared get on a horse if it hadn't been for Erin, and he was damned glad he had.

They caught up to Stormy and Erin in a few minutes, and the two horses naturally fell into the same rhythm, their hooves pounding in perfect sync as they thundered across the open field. Erin's hair was streaming behind her, and her smile lit up her face as they raced.

Steen had never seen her so relaxed, and he'd never

seen that kind of joy on her face. He realized that even as a kid, shadows had lurked in her eyes, the same ones she was still carrying. But right now, as they raced across the dried grass, he knew he was seeing the true Erin, the one who craved the simple freedom of living. It was electric, and he knew he'd never forget the pure radiance and delight on her face, or the way it felt to know that he was the one who had put it there.

She looked over at him. "Thank you," she shouted over the pounding of the hooves. "You knew what I needed."

Her appreciation was so genuine and warm that something inside him softened, as if his soul was burning just for her. As he grinned back, he began to understand that he'd been lying to himself. His plan to rebuild her sense of self-worth wasn't just for her. It was also for him. There was something about Erin that made his heart want to beat again. He needed her. He needed to touch her, to hear her laughter, and he needed to save her.

Maybe Mira had been wrong. Maybe it wasn't that he was supposed to save Erin. Maybe she was supposed to save him, the damaged ex-con who had long given up any belief that there was anything left about himself or his life that was worth saving.

What if there was something worth living for? What if there really was?

For the first time in a very long time, he felt the tiniest sliver of hope.

Chapter 9

Erin stretched out on her back on the warm, flat rock, watching the white clouds puff across the endless azure sky. Steen had taken a fleece blanket from his saddle roll and laid it over the rock, which had softened the surface, while still allowing the heat from the rock to penetrate. The moment was deliciously warm, soft, and perfect, especially since she was so aware of Steen beside her. She liked being with him, and she couldn't remember the last time she'd been so relaxed. "I think that's an ice cream cone." She pointed above their heads to a cloud that was changing shape even as she pointed it out.

Steen was stretched out beside her, taking up twice as much space as she was. His boot was resting against hers ever so lightly, and neither of them were pulling away. It was barely a touch, except that it was. Was he as aware of it as she was?

"It's a football," he said.

"Sports?" She laughed at his answer. "We're out in the most beautiful vista ever created, and you're thinking about sports?" She elbowed him playfully, just barely able to reach his side from her position on the rock. Of course he was thinking about sports. That was what had defined him through his whole life. He'd been a star football player, and had ruled the school from his athletic pedestal.

"Nope. I'm talking about sports to distract me from the fact I want to kiss you." He didn't move when he said it, and he didn't stop looking at the sky, but his words were heavy with intent. They seemed to slide beneath her clothes like a sensual caress of promise and temptation, and suddenly, she wasn't thinking about ice cream cones anymore.

Her heart began a steady thud of anticipation, but she didn't dare look at him. She didn't want to kiss him. Well, she did, more than she could practically fathom, but at the same time, there were a thousand reasons why she didn't want to, most importantly because she was terrified of how vulnerable she would be to him. He affected her more than anyone else ever had, and if she kissed him, the part of her soul that was still alive would be in his hands, at his mercy, to preserve or destroy. She was so close to the edge, so fragile, that she simply didn't have the resources to survive what Steen could do to her.

"Thinking about football isn't helping." His voice was low and rough, a seduction that was temptation beyond words. "All I can think about is what it would feel like to feel your lips against mine."

She swallowed hard. "Why is it that you want to kiss me so much?" It didn't make sense, quite frankly, and she didn't trust it. Oh, she trusted *him*, but not his need to kiss her. She wasn't the kind of woman that a man like Steen would lust after. She knew her long-standing crush on him made her more vulnerable to his attention than she might otherwise be. She didn't want her teenage fantasies to shove her into a new world of hurt, just when she was trying to regain her equilibrium from the one she'd been living in for so long.

He shrugged. "Not sure why I want to kiss you so much. Just do."

"Oh." His non-answer actually relieved her. He wasn't trying to sweet-talk her. He was simply being himself, and she was comfortable with that. She accepted his answer. He did want to kiss her, just because. She smiled up at the sky and clasped her hands behind her head. It felt so crazy to be lying in the sun with Steen, accomplishing nothing at all. "I haven't done this in a long time."

"Done what? Watched clouds? Or been coveted by a hot guy?"

She giggled. "Either of those, but I was actually just referring to the luxury of doing nothing at all."

Steen shifted, rolling onto his side toward her. He

propped his head up on his elbow, so he could see her. His cowboy hat was tipped back, but his face was still shadowed from the sun's rays. "Tell me about your life, Chambers. When you were a kid, I thought you'd go out to New York City and start running some billion-dollar company. You were so damn smart." The tiny wrinkles around the corners of his eyes indicated a man who'd spent his life outdoors, squinting in the sun. She'd spent more time indoors in a year than he'd probably spent in his life.

She smiled, running her finger over the brim of his battered hat. It was soft to touch, and she wondered how many battles it had been through with Steen. "I went to med school and became a vet." Such a short answer that didn't begin to explain all that her life had been, but that was the answer she was used to giving. No one wanted the truth, and she, quite frankly, wasn't interested in anyone knowing about it.

He nodded. "Bet your parents were proud."

"My parents?" Her chest tightened, and suddenly, the beauty of the moment vanished. "The only thing they were ever proud of me for was marrying Louis." She couldn't keep the bitterness out of her voice, or that familiar sense of failure that she'd been free of so briefly while she'd been cloud watching.

"I'm sorry to hear that. They're fools, then." Steen's voice was soft, not judging, and she sighed, realizing it felt good to have said it aloud. Maybe she did need to talk about it. Steen wasn't like the other people in her life, the ones who saw her only as an asset or something to either brag about or condemn as inadequate. Steen seemed to simply accept her for who she was, and he didn't want anything from her at all.

Except, perhaps, a kiss, and she kind of liked that he wanted that from her.

At her sigh, Steen moved closer. He set his hand on her stomach and flattened his palm across her belly, on top of her shirt.

She jumped at the unexpected contact, but when he didn't make any further movement, she relaxed again, unable to stop the happy sigh that escaped from her. "It feels good to be touched," she said softly, loving the warmth of his hand through her shirt. "It's been a long time."

"What about your husband?"

"He wasn't a toucher." She closed her eyes, noticing how Steen's palm moved with each breath she took. "We had sex a few times in the first year of our marriage, but after that, there was nothing. He didn't like to touch in public, and that soon became the way he was in private, too." She wiggled a tiny bit to her left, scooting a bit closer to Steen. Words she had kept inside for so long seemed to tumble out of her now, spilling forth from the hidden chambers of her heart. "I remember one time I came home from work, and he was sitting on the couch watching the news. I'd had a horse die on the operating table, and I was really upset. It was the first time that it had ever happened, and I was devastated."

"I can imagine." Steen's hand was warm and reassuring on her belly, and he didn't pull away upon hearing of her failure.

"I sat down next to him, sobbing, but as soon as I did, he said he needed space, and asked me to sit on the other couch." She still remembered how cool and detached his voice had been, as if he were asking a stranger to move aside in a crowd so he could pass by. For a moment, she'd been too stunned to move, shocked that he would shove her away like that when her soul was breaking. He'd repeated it twice before she'd finally understood how completely he was cutting her off. "I went into the bedroom and cried in the shower instead."

"Bastard." Steen's voice was icy, but his touch was still gentle as he began tracing circles over her belly. "What happened when he came into the bedroom? Did he say something then?"

"No, he decided to go to work instead. He said he had some research to do. I didn't see him again for a couple days because our schedules didn't overlap. He never mentioned it again, and neither did I." She sighed, suddenly needing to tell the entire, sordid story, the one she hid from everyone, including herself. "I found out later that he was having sex with one of his residents at the hospital at the time. They'd been dating for four years. Everyone knew except for me."

Steen's hand stilled. "Bastard."

She smiled at his word choice. "I can't even tell you how stupid I felt the time I decided to surprise Louis at his hospital's holiday party, and discovered that the reason he'd told me to stay away wasn't because I hated events like that, but because he was taking his girlfriend as his date." She'd never forget the moment she'd seen Louis pull the young woman into his arms for a kiss beneath the mistletoe, his hands everywhere on her body that they shouldn't have been, while his buddies cheered him on. "You should have heard the silence in that party when I walked in while Louis was making out with his girlfriend under the mistletoe. Everyone just stood there, looking at me, waiting for him to notice. It took him a full minute."

Steen swore again, choice words that brought another smile to her face. He was voicing all the words that she'd never allowed herself to feel when she'd been fighting to be strong and to pretend she didn't care. "What did he do when he noticed you?"

"Nothing. He looked up, saw me, and didn't move. He knew that if he waited long enough, I'd walk out without causing a scene." She shrugged. "He was right. What could I do? I couldn't afford a scene, and he knew it."

"I'd have caused a scene. I'm socially unacceptable like that." There was no humor in his voice, just thinly veiled outrage. He touched her jaw, turning her head toward him. His eyes were blazing with such fury that her heart turned over. She realized he had meant it completely when he'd said he would have made a scene at the party. His fury on her behalf made her throat tighten. No one had ever wanted to defend her before. No one had ever been outraged on her behalf. She prided herself on being tough, but she wasn't going to lie. It was the best feeling ever to have Steen on her side.

"Erin, you do realize that he isn't worthy of you, don't you? He isn't even worth the time it took to tell that story." He searched her face, his fingers still clasping her chin, forcing her to meet his gaze.

She couldn't help but smile, a weary smile that acknowledged his words. "I know it intellectually, but it's not always easy to remember. It makes me so angry when I think of how hard I tried all those years to get his attention, or even a little affection. He wasn't interested in me. The only reason he married me was because I was the daughter of the famous Dr. Chambers, and he wanted to learn from my dad. The fact I was on my way to becoming a vet instead of a doctor was unforgivable, but Louis and my dad felt that the benefit of becoming family outweighed the appendage of me. I know that it's his problem, not mine, but it still hurts sometimes, no matter how hard I try not to let it."

Steen said nothing, but his hand began to move again across her stomach, gentle touching that seemed to take away that isolation that had plagued her for so long. "They're fools," he finally said. "Being a vet is amazing, and it's exactly what you should be doing."

She smiled at his support, hearing the truth in his voice. "When my dad found out that Louis had been having an affair for four years, you know what he said to me?"

His hand stilled as he looked at her. "What?"

"He said that it was my fault because how could Louis be expected to be fulfilled by a woman like me? He forgave Louis, and hated me for forcing Louis to do it." She managed a small laugh, trying to keep herself from caring. "I felt so stupid. I'd tried so hard to impress all of them my whole life, and I failed. Once my dad said that, and my mom agreed with him, I finally understood the truth. I realized I'd never be enough for them. I saw how stupid I'd been trying to win the approval of people who will never see it." She sighed and wrapped her hand around Steen's wrist, needing to ground herself in him. "After my divorce, I spent about a year burying myself in my work, but I was dying inside. That's why I came out here to help Josie. I needed to get away. I don't even know who I am anymore, Steen. I've spent my whole life trying to be good enough, and I'm not. So, if I stop trying, then who am I? I don't even know."

Steen sighed, and he bent over her, his blue eyes searching her face. "Listen to me, Erin. I know all about people who will use you for what they want. You can never win them over. You have to simply cut them out of your life and do what you want. You'll never win that battle."

"I'm learning that," she said. "But I need the reminder…a lot."

"No problem. I'll hammer it into you." His face became more serious. "Don't let them take away who you are. Never give anyone that power."

His voice was hard and bitter, and she thought back to

all the rumors that had surrounded him as a child. She cocked her head, noticing the small scar above his left eyebrow. "Was your dad as horrible as everyone said? Is that who betrayed you?"

He shrugged noncommittally, as if the question didn't matter to him. "He was an abusive alcoholic who knocked up women as fast as he could. He allowed all his bastards to run around the house trying to find food while he drank, smoked, and took his hatred of life out on all of us, so yeah, not a good guy. He had no expectations for any of us, except to get out of his way, or to be target practice for his fists."

She felt her jaw drop open. "Really? He punched you?"

"When I was little, he did, but when I got bigger, no." He flexed his arm mockingly. "One of the advantages of being in prime physical condition is that an out of shape bum can't push you around, even when you're fifteen."

She felt like such a complainer. Her heart broke for what he'd endured, and for the casual way he blew it off. There was no way a child could endure that and not bear the scars on his heart. "I'm so sorry. Your situation was so much worse than mine. I had no idea what you were going through—"

"No. Don't belittle yourself." He leaned over her again, his face intense as he stared at her. "My life was easier, because by the time I came to live with him full-time, I knew he was a bastard and I didn't care what he thought. I stayed out of his way and lived my life. Your parents controlled you from the time you were a baby, and that's a hell of a lot harder to deal with. Conditional love is more destructive than no love, because they can use it to manipulate and destroy you. Just because they didn't shove cigarettes into your arm doesn't mean they weren't equally as shitty."

Her heart turned. "Your dad burned you with his cigarettes?"

"Once. I never let him do it again." There was a hardness to Steen's face that made her shiver. He may have been her childhood crush and the only boy in school that made her feel noticed, but there was a side to him that was so tough and hard, a world she had no experience with at all.

"I'm so sorry." She reached up and pressed her hand to his face. His whiskers prickled her palm, but she didn't mind.

"You deserved so much more, Steen. I'm so glad that you were able to find your path and find a life with people who do see your value."

Something flickered in his eyes, something dark and dangerous.

He didn't answer, but instead, he took her hand and pressed his lips to her palm, tracing kisses across her skin. One kiss. Then another. Then another.

The moment he felt her hand against his lips, Steen knew he was lost. No one had ever looked at him the way Erin did, as if her heart was breaking for his pain. No one had ever assumed that he was the good guy that had found his path. He was so used to being the scum, and he knew that with his prison record, that would follow him throughout his life.

He had a feeling he should tell Erin about his stint in prison so she wouldn't hate him when she found out how wrong she'd been about him, but he couldn't bring himself to do it. He desperately needed her to look at him like he was a worthwhile human being. He'd thought he was long past caring what anyone thought about him, but he'd been wrong. He needed Erin to think he was okay, and he needed it with every fiber of his soul.

He couldn't break this moment, and this connection by poisoning it with who he really was. He wanted to be the guy who Erin saw when she looked at him, and he wanted to erase all the damage her parents and her ex had done to her.

She was watching him carefully, her gaze riveted to his as he kissed her palm. "That feels really good," she whispered.

"It's supposed to." He kissed the underside of her wrist, then pressed another kiss slightly further along her arm. "Touching is good."

She shook her head. "My family never hugged, and Louis never touched me. I'm not used to it. I didn't think I needed it." Her eyes were wide and vulnerable as she watched him. "But my whole body is crying out for you right now."

Her words were so honest and vulnerable that they seemed to plunge right past his shields, deep into the part of him that he'd shut down for so long. He went still, staring at her, searching her face for some kind of deception or manipulation, but there was nothing. Just stark honesty and need. He swore under his breath as he released her hand and leaned over her. He pressed a light kiss to her cheek.

Her eyes fluttered shut, and she put her hand over his, where it was still resting on her belly. "Why are you doing this?" she whispered, her voice breathy and shaky.

"Because I need to. I need to wipe away all the taint from your parents and Louis, and I need to feel what it's like to be with the one woman on this earth who has a good soul." He kissed the corner of her mouth, barely able to keep himself from rolling on top of her and taking her the way he wanted to. They were alone out in the wilderness, and their horses were tethered nearby. There was no one around for miles, and he knew that they had complete privacy under the brilliant blue sky that he'd barely seen for those four years in prison. "Tell me no," he said, kissing the other side of her mouth. "Tell me to stop. I won't stop on my own, but I know you deserve so much more than me."

Her eyes opened. "What do I deserve?"

He lightly bit her lower lip, then traced the tip of his tongue across it. "You deserve to feel like you are the sexiest, most treasured, and most brilliant woman on the face of the earth." He kissed along her jaw toward her ear. "You deserve to be kissed like the world will stop turning if the kiss ever ends." He grazed his teeth over her earlobe. "You deserve to be kissed by a man who makes you feel like there is no woman on earth who will ever, ever, matter to him, except for you."

Her fingers tightened around his hand. "Steen."

He pulled back far enough to look at her. "Yeah?"

"That's how you make me feel."

He went still, his heart suddenly thundering through him. He knew then that he was going to have to tell her right then, right there, who he really was and what he'd done. It didn't matter that he'd lose out on the way she looked at him. There was no way he was going to be one more black mark on her soul by betraying her. Swearing, he pulled back. "I'm not that guy, Erin. I swear, I'm not that guy. I can't be what you deserve—"

She put her finger over his lips, silencing him. "I know you have secrets, Steen. So do I. But right now, do they matter? Can't this moment just be what it is? I know who you are in your soul, and you see me for who I am. Isn't that enough?" Her eyes were shining with unshed tears. "Can't you just be who you are for now? Can't we forget about all the baggage and secrets, and put them aside for this moment? Can't you just kiss me? Please? I want this moment with you. It's the only way I'll ever know what it's supposed to be like to be kissed by someone who actually wants me just for me. I don't want anyone else. Just you."

Something shifted inside him, something that broke through his need to shield her from who he really was and made him want to be that guy, for her, right now. He knew that he saw in her things that no one else saw. He *knew* that. Yeah, he'd stand back and let her go home in ten days, but she knew she was leaving as well, so there were limits to what she could expect of this, and of him, especially when it came to a promise of forever. Could ten days change her life? His?

She smiled and slid her hands behind his neck, gently tugging him closer. "Face it, Steen, you need this as much as I do. There's always been something between us, and we both know it." She traced her fingers on the back of his neck, a gesture so tender and seductive that it almost broke him.

He had two choices right now. Get on his horse and get as far away as he could from her, or kiss her the way he wanted to.

There was no way he was going to reject her, not when what she wanted from him was exactly what he wanted to give her. He slid his free hand behind her head, tangling his fingers in her hair. "If you had any idea how much I want you, you'd never offer yourself up like this," he said softly, flicking the hem of her shirt aside so that his palm was spread on her bare skin.

Her stomach shuddered under his touch, and she sucked in her breath. "The fact that you want to touch me is the most incredible feeling," she said. "The fact you want me is... amazing."

"Oh, sweetheart, you have no idea." He finally succumbed to the need that had been coursing through him for so long, and he kissed her. It wasn't a chaste, innocent kiss. He was long past being able to do that. It was a kiss with no boundaries, a kiss that shattered any last remnant of resistance, a kiss that promised every inch of his soul.

Chapter 10

The moment Steen kissed her, Erin felt like everything she understood about the world had shattered. His kiss was so intense, so demanding, so incredibly intoxicating that she knew instantly that she was being kissed by a man who had never lived behind walls like those that had constrained her for so long.

He kissed her with an untamed, unashamed intensity that held nothing back. His lips were hot and demanding, coaxing her to let him in. The moment she parted her lips to kiss him back, he invaded her mouth with his tongue, a seductive, sensual assault that streaked through her body, tearing her from its protective, dead shell and catapulting her into a world of sensation and emotion that she'd never felt before.

She wrapped her arms around his neck, holding on desperately as she kissed him back, swept into passion so intense she could barely even think, let alone resist it. As he kissed her, he slid his hand across her torso, caressing every inch. His fingers brushed against the underside of her breast, and she almost gasped at the intensity of the sensation.

He gave her no time to react, and before she knew what he'd done, he'd unhooked the front clasp of her bra. Her breasts fell free, and exhilaration rushed through her at the sensation of being utterly free from constraint. He cupped her left breast and thumbed her nipple. The bud became hard instantly, and she squirmed, barely able to stand the intensity of her response to him.

"Sit up for a sec." His voice was low and thick as he

grabbed her hands and pulled her upright.

She barely had time to find her balance before he'd grabbed her shirt and pulled it and her bra over her head. Embarrassment flooded her cheeks when his gaze went to her breasts, but before she could hide them, his face softened with such emotion that she was no longer afraid.

"They're beautiful," he whispered as he bent his head and pressed a kiss to each breast, his kiss so tender that she wanted to cry.

She ran her fingers through his hair. "How are you like this? How do you make me feel so beautiful and appealing? And wanted?"

He sat up, put his hands on her hips, and pulled her onto his lap. She wrapped her legs around his waist, faintly embarrassed to be sitting on his lap half-naked while they were outside in plain sight of anyone who happened by. At the same time, she felt wildly exhilarated to feel the breeze and the warm sun on her back, and the press of his erection against the juncture of her thighs through her jeans.

"Because I think you're amazing," he said. "I'm just letting you feel what I feel." Then, before she could talk more, he kissed her again, deeply, passionately, like a man who had been starved for her touch and couldn't go one more minute without her.

His hands were all over her upper body, tracing along her spine, cupping her breasts, and even sliding down over her hips to her butt. The sensation of skin on skin was incredible, and she wanted more. She wanted to touch him like he was touching her, to feel his skin beneath her palms, to taste him the way he was tasting her.

"Go ahead," he whispered against her ear. "Do it."

She realized suddenly that she'd been gripping the hem of his shirt, her fingers nearly shredding the material she was holding it so hard. "Is it okay?"

Steen laughed under his breath as he pulled back from her. "Sweetheart, it's more than okay." He peeled her hand from his shirt and pressed it to the front of his jeans. "Feel that?"

Her cheeks turned red. "Yes."

"That's your green light. You can do anything you

want to me." He framed her face. "I'm not like Louis," he said, searching her face. "There's no chance on God's green earth that I would *ever* prefer to have your hands off my body instead of on it. Do you understand? I want this. I want your kiss. I want your touch. I want you to feel how amazing you are and how much I want you."

She stared at him in wonderment. "You mean that."

"Hell, yeah, I mean it." With a low groan, he released her face, grabbed the hem of his shirt, and ripped it over his head, just as he'd done in the barn. But this time, she wasn't looking at him as a patient. She was seeing him as a man, a man she'd been in love with since she was fourteen years old, a man who *wanted* her to touch him.

After growing up with parents who never hugged and living with a husband who'd banished her from physical proximity, let alone intimacy, it was so foreign to be with a man who didn't shut her out.

Tentatively, almost afraid he was going to stop her, she ran her fingers across his chest. His muscles were cut and defined, despite how lean he was, and she could only imagine the raw breadth of him when he hadn't been weeks from almost dying. She brushed her fingers through the hair on his chest, tracing its path toward the waistband of his jeans. His stomach tightened as she ran her fingers across his abs, and she felt the rock hard muscles beneath his skin. She glanced up at his face and saw he was watching her with smoldering eyes, as if he were doing everything in his power not to tear the rest of her clothes off and plunge right into her.

Exhilaration rippled through her, and a heady sense of empowerment. She worked her way back up his chest, then lightly pushed on him. "Lie down." His body was so rigid with need that she didn't expect him to acquiesce.

In fact, for a brief moment, all he did was quirk one eyebrow at her. "You're bossing me around?"

"I'm trying."

He grinned then, and stretched back on the rock, clasping his hands behind his head. "I'm all yours, sweetheart, but I have to warn you, at some point, you're going to push me beyond my limit."

She grinned in anticipation as she straddled his hips. His erection was straining against his jeans, and she instinctively shifted so it was pressing into her exactly where she wanted it. She couldn't quite contain her small gasp when she got her position right. "Then what happens?"

His eyes were hooded as he watched her. "Then I'm the boss."

Oh, wow, she kind of liked the sound of that. Grinning, she braced her hands on either side of his head and kissed him. She'd meant for it to be flirty and teasing, but the moment their lips came together, the kiss turned ravenous. She immediately forgot about being the seductress, and could think only about how much she wanted to be close to him.

He cupped her breasts, then broke the kiss and pulled her upward, so that he could take her nipple into his mouth. Desire rushed through her as he sucked and bit, and she tipped her head back, drinking in every feeling he was awakening in her. This was Steen, the man she'd idolized for so long. It was surreal to be touched so hungrily, by a man she craved so deeply. It was beyond anything she could have imagined, and she'd spent a lot of time imagining what it could have been like if she'd married someone else, anyone else, other than Louis. But never had she imagined it could be like this.

Still kissing her breasts, Steen's hands went to the fly of her jeans. She sucked in her belly when he unbuttoned them, and her heart started racing as he slowly unzipped them. Could she do this? Sleep with Steen? "I don't think—"

She cut herself off when he slid his hands over her hips, dragging her jeans and underwear down. His hands felt amazing on her hips, and the way he slid them over her thighs, like he wanted to own them, was exhilarating. She felt his possessiveness in every move he made, and she loved it.

Excitement rushed through her, and without thinking, she began to unbutton his jeans. He helped her, and within moments, the sensual kissing had been consumed by a frantic need for bare skin, without clothing in the way. She was vaguely aware of jeans going flying, and boots thudding off the rock to the ground below, but the sheer strength of Steen's presence obscured everything else from her mind.

This time, when he sat up and pulled her onto his lap, there were no thick pieces of denim between them. Just the unbelievable sensation of skin against skin, of his body against hers. His erection pressed against her belly as she wrapped her arms around his neck, kissing him so desperately, as if she could pour her entire soul into his. His response was equally intense, his hands spanning her lower back, then her hips, then her rear end, as if he needed to touch every part of her at once just to survive.

"I want to be inside you," he whispered.

Her heart leapt. Really? Was this really going to happen? "Me, too."

"I don't have any condoms."

She pulled back, her cheeks flooding. "I'm on the pill. Not because I'm having sex with anyone, because I'm not, but it's for cramps." God, did he think she did this all the time?

His expression softened, as if he'd read her mind. "Sweetheart, you could carry around entire cartons of condoms and sixteen different sexual aids, and I still wouldn't think you slept around." He grabbed her hips, pulling her closer. "I'm clean. When I was dying in the hospital, they tested me for every disease known to mankind. One of those invasions of privacy they do in pris—" He cut himself off, his face suddenly going hard.

She didn't know what he'd just thought of, but her heart wanted to cry for the sudden flash of torment in his face. She pressed a kiss to his mouth, refusing to give up until he responded. After a moment of hesitation, he grabbed her hair and turned the kiss carnal, as if he were running from whatever memory had just flared up. It was bruising, almost overwhelming, but instead of turning her off, his desperation seemed to ignite something inside her, something feral and wild, a side of her that she'd never before allowed to be free.

Their upper bodies were crushed against each other, her breasts smashed against his bare chest, her legs tight around his hips. She was trying to keep her thigh away from his injured side, but she could barely keep her focus as the kisses and touching intensified. Finally, desperately, she tried to break away to speak, but he barely gave her room to get the words out. "Me, too," she managed, before he kissed her again, so deeply and intimately it felt as if he were a part of her soul. "After Louis cheated..." Another kiss, deeper, more intense. His hands on her butt, gripping her. "I had to know. I got tested..."

"I don't give a shit if you have a thousand diseases," Steen said as he grabbed her hips and lifted her up. "Whatever happens after this moment doesn't matter. I'd give my life if it was the only way I could have this moment with you."

His eyes were intense and heated as he stared at her, and her heart tightened when she realized he meant every word. "Steen—"

"You're mine, Erin, and you always have been." And with that statement, he lowered her down onto his erection.

He slid inside perfectly, and she gasped when he filled her. He was so deep, deeper than she'd ever felt, and it was incredible. Tears filled her eyes as he moved her hips in a rhythm that brought him deeper and deeper, locking them together in a way that she knew would be imprinted upon her soul forever.

She wrapped her arms around his neck and kissed him, a searing kiss that consumed them both. She began to move on him, and his hips moved as well, tantalizing her with each thrust and tease. Desire pooled in her belly, building and building until she felt like her body was going to explode. She was gripping his shoulders, her entire body tense. "You can go ahead," she said, even as she was gasping for air. She didn't want him to wait for her, for the orgasm that would never come. What she was experiencing was beyond what she had ever expected, and she didn't want it ruined by both of them trying to get her to have an orgasm that would never happen. "I never have them."

"Never?" There was a low chuckle. "You've never been with me, sweetheart." He somehow managed to thrust even deeper, despite the fact that he was sitting up and she was on his lap.

She gasped, her finger digging into his shoulders. "Please don't put that kind of pressure on me," she said. "It will just ruin it. I want it to be perfect—"

He moved his hand between them and touched her clitoris. She yelped at the rush of sensation, and suddenly, she couldn't think, she couldn't breathe, she couldn't do anything but hold onto him as he rubbed the taut bud, his fingers sliding over the nub again and again, until her whole body was screaming for release.

"Now," he whispered, just before he lifted her up and thrust deep inside her again.

The orgasm exploded through her, a searing release that seemed to ignite every cell of her body. She gasped his name, but he swallowed her yelp in a blistering kiss as he came, his hips pounding into her as he poured his seed into her body, his arms wrapped so tightly around her she didn't even bother to hold herself up. She just gave herself completely over to the orgasm, to him, to the utter capitulation of her soul, until there was nothing left but one final shudder as she collapsed against him.

For a long while, they didn't move. They simply stayed entwined, with her leaning against him while he held her up. He laughed softly, nuzzling her neck as he locked his arms around her back, not letting her go. "Never?" he teased. "Did you say you *never* had them? Because I'm pretty sure that's what you said."

She sighed, smiling into his neck as she rested her hands limply on his hips. "Apparently, I lied."

"Apparently. I forgive you, this one time." He pressed his lips to her forehead, and she could feel the laughter rumbling in his chest. "But never do it again."

"Have an orgasm?" she teased. "Or lie?"

He slid his hand beneath her chin, lifting her head so she was looking at him. "Sweetheart, if I have anything to say about it, there are going to be a lot more orgasms in your future. Hundreds. Thousands. Maybe even millions."

There was no way to stop the thrill of anticipation. "A million? How am I going to take care of all the animals?"

He grinned. "We have time."

At his words, her smile faded. "Ten days," she said. "We only have ten days."

His smile faded as well, and for a long moment, there was only silence between them. Finally, he brushed the hair back from her face. "A million in ten days is going to take a lot of work." His voice was rough, now, almost hoarse. "We better get busy, don't you think?" He tugged lightly on her hair. "I know it's just a bunk house, but I think you should stay with me tonight." His smile was completely gone now, and his expression was serious. "I mean it. Stay with me tonight."

The thought of crawling into bed with him, and waking up in his arms was intoxicating, but instead of excitement, Erin just felt a deep sense of loneliness settling down around her. She knew she had to leave in ten days. It was her choice to do so. It was her career, and her life. She didn't want Steen trying to stop her from living her life, but at the same time, she realized she was a little bit crushed that he hadn't issued even the slightest hint at having this thing they'd started go beyond the ten days, not even a whisper of remorse that it would have to end. Just a request to spend the night so that they could make the most of the ten days before it was over.

His eyes narrowed. "What did I say?"

"Nothing." She managed a smile as she raised herself off him and tried to stand up.

He caught her around the waist, rolled her onto her back on the rock, and pinned her down with his body. "No." His eyes were blazing again, as they had been every other time she'd tried to shut him out. "You don't share something as intimate as what we just shared and then lock me out. What just happened?"

She shook her head and pushed ineffectually at his arm. "Nothing. I just want to go."

Trying to budge him was like trying to move a mountain with a feather. He just settled more deeply on her, pinning her to the rock. Yes, he was lean from his injury, but even so, he was so much heavier and stronger than she was. She had no chance of extricating herself until he decided to let her go. "Steen, please, this isn't fair. I want to go."

He still didn't move. "You remember the girl I was dating in high school?"

She hesitated, trying to grasp the sudden change of topic. "Rachel? Yes, of course." She'd hated that red-haired cheerleader with every ounce of her soul. The girl had fondled Steen constantly, but she'd been mean and nasty to Erin every time they were alone. She had no idea what she'd done to make Rachel dislike her, but the cheerleader had been very good at punishing her for it.

"When I busted my knee in high school, she decided that I wasn't going anywhere, and she was done with me."

Erin frowned, remembering how they'd broken up in senior year. "Well, she wasn't very nice—"

"You know how I found out?" He met her gaze, and this time, she saw real emotion in them. Betrayal. Hurt. Pain. "I walked into her house to take her to dinner for our three-year anniversary, and she was messing around with the backup quarterback who had taken over for me when I got hurt. She laughed and said I was a fool not to realize what was going on, and that everyone knew." His voice was bitter.

Erin's heart tightened. "I'm sorry." She knew how awful that was. There was no pain that bit as deeply as having the person you loved and trusted most betray you.

He met her gaze again. "I didn't learn my lesson well enough that time," he said. "Five years ago, I ran into her at the local grocery store. She was in town for a wedding. I was in a bad place in my life, and I saw her as a sign from the angels. She talked a good game, and asked for forgiveness for what she'd done to me in high school. I believed she'd changed, and I thought she regretted it. I thought she had been sent to me to drag me back to the land of the living. We were in the middle of having sex when her husband walked into the hotel room. She had used me to make him jealous because she was pissed at him. She told him that I—" He stopped then, his face going hard.

She held her breath, fear prickling down her spine. Something terrible had happened that night, she was certain. Something that had eviscerated him. "What happened, Steen?"

He shook his head. "The day my mom left me at my dad's," he said, changing the subject again, "she told me that she'd be back in a week, like she had been every other time. I waited for her. Day after day after day. I believed she would come back for me, but she never did. I never heard from her again. She made me a promise to be there for me, just like Rachel had, and they both lied. So, I learned my lesson about believing in anyone, and I learned it well. I don't trust women, and I don't trust secrets." He searched her face. "But I trust you, Erin. You're the only person on this God-forsaken planet that I trust, and I can't take it if you lie to me and shut me out."

There was an edge to his voice, something desperate, something far beyond the story he'd told about Rachel. What else had happened that night in the hotel room? "Steen—"

"Tell me what's wrong, Erin. I want to know what I did to make you pull away." He looked stricken, almost tormented. "Did I read the signs wrong? Did you not want to make love? Did I talk you into something you didn't want to do?"

"Oh, God, no. I wanted you to make love to me more than anything else I've ever wanted." She was horrified that she'd made him wonder that.

Relief rushed across his face, and she felt his body tremble as he bowed his head for a moment, gathering himself.

"I'm so sorry," she said. "I never meant to make you think that." She instinctively touched his head, running her fingers through his hair.

He looked up, searching her face, as if he were waiting for her to say the rest. "You can tell me anything, Erin. I've known you since we were kids." He pressed a kiss to her left breast, just above her heart. "Please tell me why you're pulling away. I don't know what I did. I need to know."

"I just..." God, how could she say the truth without sounding like a desperate fool?

"You just what?" He caught her hand and kissed her palm.

She watched him kiss her. His jaw was rough with stubble, unlike the first time she'd seen him when he'd been so clean-shaven, with his hair super short. It had been only a week and a half, but his hair was a little longer, and he looked rougher. The bones in his shoulders were protruding too much through skin that didn't have enough fat. His shoulder had an old surgical scar across it, and his side was bandaged. His cheeks were more hollow than they had once been. He was a man who had been through tough things, things that still haunted him. He was a man who had truly lived, and he made her want to live as well.

The person she'd been her whole life would never speak up about what was in her heart, for fear of upsetting or disappointing him. But he made her want to be brave, and not hide from who she was or what she felt. "When I said that we only had ten days..." She stopped, and bit her lip. Dammit. She didn't want to sound needy and pathetic. What if it drove him away?

His eyebrow quirked. "Yeah?"

She cleared her throat, forcing herself to continue. "You didn't seem to care that we only had ten days, other than trying to figure out how to fit in as much sex as possible." There, she said it. Well, she hadn't exactly spelled it out, but she'd said enough.

His face darkened, and he pulled back, his body tensing.

The moment he withdrew, she knew she'd made a mistake. The reason he hadn't mentioned anything after ten days was because *he didn't want it*. She shouldn't have said anything. Damn him for making her say it!

But it was too late. There was no taking it back.

Chapter 11

Steen saw the hurt in Erin's eyes, and he felt it in the sudden softness of her voice. Regret poured through him. Son of a bitch. This wasn't supposed to happen this way. He was supposed to rebuild her, not tear her down.

"Never mind." She pushed ineffectually at his shoulders, but he didn't move off her. "Forget I said it. It's fine. I'm leaving. I get it—"

"No, you don't." He knew he was being a bastard by using his weight to keep her from leaving, but he knew that if she got up, she'd shut him out and disappear from his life. There was no way he could let her run away from him, not before he'd had the chance to make this right.

She glared at him, her chin held stiffly. "I don't what?"

"You don't get it."

"Oh, really? What don't I get?" Her voice was cool and distant, and he knew it was his fault.

Swearing, he struggled to think of how to phrase it. The last thing he wanted was to let her walk out of his life after ten days. It had been only a few days since they'd reconnected, and he couldn't get her out of his mind for even a split second. After another ten days, letting her go would be like carving out his own heart with a pitchfork and leaving it in the hot sun to fry, but he knew he had to do it. She was better than his world, and she didn't deserve to be trapped in his life. He couldn't ask her to stay, but he couldn't go with her, for a whole host of reasons, including the fact that she deserved more than to be saddled with him. There was no future for them, but he, somehow, had to make her understand that it wasn't *her* that was the issue.

"Steen!" She smacked his shoulder lightly. "Let's just let it go. The sex was great. We finally did it. I need to get back to work—"

"Stop it!" He grabbed her wrist, anger roiling through him. "Don't talk like that. It wasn't sex. It was much more than that." Then he paused…sudden fear knifing through him. What if he was wrong? What if he was the only one who'd thought it was more? "Wasn't it? Or was that all it was to you? Sex?"

Her mouth opened, and then closed. Confusion flickered across her face. "I don't understand you. What do you want from me?"

"What do I want?" Swearing, he finally rolled off her. "I don't want anything *from* you. I just wanted to rebuild you after that piece of shit tore you down."

"What?" She sat up and grabbed her bra and shirt from the pile nearby. "That's why you had sex with me? As part of a restoration project or something?"

"Shit, no." He ran his hand through his hair. Hell, he was making a mockery of this. What the hell was he supposed to say to make this right? "I haven't been with a woman in years. It's not worth it to me. There's no other woman on this planet that I would have made love to today except for you. No one."

She paused with her shirt half on, staring at him. "What are you trying to say, Steen? I don't understand."

Swearing, he turned toward her. "The first time I noticed you was on the third day of my junior year. You were in eighth grade, still in middle school, and you crossed the street to the other side when you saw me walking with my friends."

Her eyes narrowed. "You and your friends were loud and obnoxious. You scared me. I always avoided you guys…until you started being different."

Guilt shot through him at the memories of the guy he had once been. "I watched you cross the street, and as soon as you got there, you stopped and knelt down. There was a baby bird that had fallen out of a nest. Do you remember?"

She blinked, her forehead wrinkled in confusion. "You were there that day?"

"Yeah, I was." He'd never forget it either. "You picked it up and made a nest for it on the handlebars of your bike. Then, you rode off down the street with it." He had been so fascinated by the gentle way she'd handled the bird. He'd never seen anyone touch a living creature with such care. "I followed you. I wanted to see where you were going."

Her eyebrows went up. "You *followed* me?"

"Yeah. You went to the nearest vet. They were closed, but you banged on the door until the vet came out. You remember what happened?"

She sat back on her heels. "Of course I do. I argued with her until she took the bird. That's when I decided to be a vet, so I could help animals"

He leaned forward. "No, that's not what happened. What happened was that she said it would cost at least five hundred dollars to treat the bird, and that if you got money from your mother, she would take care of the bird. You said your mother wouldn't pay, so she said she wouldn't help you." He would never forget the absolute determination on Erin's face, or the way she'd clenched her skinny little fists. "You said you'd work for her, and she said you were too young. So, then you said you'd trade your bike."

Erin's eyes widened. "You heard that whole exchange?"

"Hell, yeah. I thought the vet was a bitch for taking your bike. I saw you crying when you handed it over, but you never hesitated. You walked everywhere for the rest of the year." He touched her cheek softly. "You were a rich kid whose parents refused to give you a new bike. You knew that would happen, but you gave your bike away anyway to save that little bird. I'd never seen anyone do anything selfless like that in my life. I had no idea that people like you existed." He wrapped a strand of her hair around his finger. "You changed my worldview that day. There were many times in my life, especially during the last four years, when thinking of you was the only damn thing that kept me going. If you think for one second that I'd ever dishonor you by using your body, then I've completely fucked up, because all I want to do is make you understand that there's no one else in this damn world that matters except for you."

She stared at him, her mouth parted slightly, her shirt

still only halfway on. She didn't say anything, and he couldn't tell what she was thinking.

"Don't you get it?" He shook his head, struggling with how to make her understand how much he valued her. "My mother ditched me at my dad's when I was twelve. She'd promised she was going to come back, like she always had before, but this time, she never did. She just disappeared. I didn't belong with my brothers, because they'd grown up there. I believed in her, and she abandoned me to a bastard who kicked the shit out of me. My brothers were almost strangers. I rode horses and played football, trying to be so impressive that I didn't need anyone. And then you showed me that sometimes, people are just kind for no reason at all. Do you understand what you gave me? What you showed me?" He spread his hands, showing all the scars on his knuckles from his father, from sports, and from horses. "This is my life, and yet you make me forget about it all."

He hadn't planned to tell her that she was the foundation that had kept him going his entire life. He knew he hadn't explained it adequately, but he didn't have better words to describe it.

Erin finished pulling her shirt on, then scooted over to him. She sat in front of him, searching his face. "You were the only person who ever, *ever* looked at me like I was special. I didn't know that you saw that thing with the bird, but the expression on your face every time you looked at me was an incredible gift. You're the reason I'm a vet and not a famous doctor. You made me feel like I was worth something just by being me. You never wanted anything from me. Ever. You just smiled at me with kindness."

He framed her face with his hands, the tight ache in his heart easing. "That's all I want," he said softly. "For you to realize how amazing you are. If I can give you that, then I now understand why it wasn't my time to die in that hospital."

Tears filled her eyes. "Why don't you care what happens after ten days? Why doesn't it bother you I'm going to leave? Why don't you want to ask me to stay?"

He closed his eyes against the urge to ask her exactly the same question. Why did she want to leave? Why did she want to return to the world that had treated her so badly? The need to drag her into his world was almost overwhelming, and he had to fight not to do it. Finally, he opened his eyes. She was staring at him, her eyes wide, waiting for his answer.

"I'll break you, if you stay with me," he said finally.

She frowned. "What? What does that mean?"

He brushed the hair back from her face. "My secrets are very bad, Erin. You won't be able to look at me the same way once you know them, and you won't be able to live with them."

She raised her brows. "Why don't you let me make that choice?"

"Because I wouldn't be able to handle it if you looked at me like I was a monster," he said quietly. "The way you look at me is all that gets me through each day. I can't afford to lose that. I can't afford for you to see me the way the rest of the world does. If you stay, you'll find out, and I don't want that."

She bit her lip, searching his face. "You're judging me," she said softly. "You think I can't see past it. That's not believing in me."

"No, it's because I do believe in you." He took her hands. "You deserve more than I could ever give you, and you would realize it. You burn for me because you've never been loved and desired this way. Once you get used to it, you'll be ready for more, for a man who can offer you more than his insatiable need for your body and your soul. I won't trap you in my life." He traced his finger over her mouth. "Sometimes the people who come into your life are supposed to stay in it forever. Other times, their impact on you is what lasts, and they're meant to become a part of your life story, and your past."

Tears brimmed in her eyes, but she pulled back, out of his reach. "I'll never force myself on someone, including you" she said stiffly. "I deserve more. I deserve someone who wants me."

He nodded. "Yeah, you do." He wanted to tell her that *he* was that guy, the one who wanted her with every fiber of his soul, but he didn't. He had to let her go. *He had to.* So he didn't move as she retrieved the rest of her clothes, watching as all that skin disappeared under layers of cotton, designed to shut him out. She climbed down from the rock to get her boots, not even looking at him.

He knew that he was losing her, but he didn't speak up. She needed to be strong enough to walk away from something that wasn't enough for her, so he wasn't going to stop her, but at the same time, he hated the fact that she was walking away hurt. He couldn't stand knowing that he'd hurt her, but as hell was his witness, he didn't want to tell her the truth. He couldn't risk it.

But as she untied her horse and swung up into the saddle, he couldn't stop thinking about whether he could risk not telling her the truth. What if she did understand? What if she was able to see past it? Then, she would understand why he couldn't be with her, and maybe they could part without her being hurt...and maybe, just maybe...she would still look at him the same way, even knowing exactly who he was. What were the odds? Slim? None? He couldn't risk it. But at the same time, would he ever forgive himself for not trying?

Chapter 12

Erin pushed her horse hard on the way back to the ranch. She buried her hurt in the wind tearing through her hair, and in the sound of Stormy's hooves thundering on the parched ground. She let the strength of the animal fill her, and she let the speed tear a lifetime of vulnerability from her. She hated herself for letting Steen hurt her. She hated Steen for hiding secrets from her. Withholding his truth felt almost as bad as when Louis had withheld physical affection from her, because she'd believed in the connection she and Steen had.

She screamed her frustration as they galloped across the meadow, furious at herself for being so pathetic that she let so many people hurt her and manipulate her. She'd run away from her life and her job to hide out in Wyoming, and yet, she was the same person she'd been in Virginia. She was still afraid to fight for what she wanted. She still let people cut her out. She still cried silent tears when she was hurt.

She didn't want to be like this anymore.

The wind blew the tears from her cheeks as she urged the horse onward, trusting the animal to know the way home.

She was still riding hard when the ranch came into view. She was so startled by the vista that she reined Stormy in so she could get a better look. When they'd ridden away earlier, she hadn't looked back and gotten a good view. But now...it was breathtaking. The ranch house was a picturesque expanse of glass and windows, stretching across the crest of the hill. She could imagine how incredible the view was at sunset, looking out across the land, which seemed to stretch on forever.

The house looked over the three barns, which were all well-kept and impressive. A sizeable bunkhouse sat behind the barns, sunk lower behind a hill. It had no scenic view, except of the immediate area, but she still felt the immense peace of the place. In the distance, she could see animals grazing, bound by rustic wooden fences and some wire ones. Beyond the ranch, she could see the driveway leading down toward the road, but from her vantage point, she couldn't see the road. All she could see was land, animals, and the ranch buildings.

She took a deep breath, and she felt the frantic pace of her heart slow, eased by the sheer magnitude of peace that the earth seemed to breathe into her. It was pure simplicity. No fancy cars. No standards to live up to. No one who cared about anything other than taking care of animals and living from the earth.

She inhaled again, and this time, for the first time in what felt like years, she felt her lungs expand fully, taking in air that she'd never had room for.

Behind her came the steady rhythm of hoof beats, but she didn't turn around. She also didn't try to run away.

Steen rode up beside her, and reined in to a halt beside her. He said nothing, but sat astride, surveying the same vista that she was looking at it.

"It's beautiful," she said finally. "I can't believe you live here. I can feel all my stress melting away."

"The bunkhouse is just temporary," he said. "This hill we're on is my hill. If I want to build a house here, this is my spot."

She looked over at him, surprised by his comment. "*If* you want to build here? Why wouldn't you?"

He said nothing for a long moment, still staring across the field. "Because I don't belong. This is my brother's place."

She frowned. "He doesn't want you to live here?"

"No, he does. He wants all the Stockton brothers to set up homesteads. He wants us all to live together as a happy family."

She couldn't decipher the inflection of his words, and she studied his face, trying to understand what he wasn't saying.

"You don't want to?"

He finally looked at her. "I didn't grow up with them. I was never a part of the group. Chase has always reached out to me, and I trust him, but I don't know the others. It's not my right to live here."

The defensive shield she'd erected so quickly around her heart seemed to weaken at his words. "It seems to me if Chase believes you have a right to live here, then you might."

"No." He took a deep breath. "I need to stay away from them for the same reason I need to stay away from you. I'm not a good guy."

She turned her horse so she could face him, her heart starting to pound. "And why do you say that?"

He met her gaze, and she saw the tension in his jaw. "My goal was to rebuild you, not hurt you, Erin. That's all that matters to me. If my withholding of the truth hurts you, then it's not the right decision." He took a deep breath, and she knew suddenly that he was going to tell her. He didn't want to, but he was going to.

And that was enough.

She held up her hand to stop him. "It's okay, Steen. I don't need to know."

His brow furrowed. "You do need to know—"

"No, I don't." She urged her horse over to him. "I know how much you don't want to tell me, but you're willing to do it to make me feel better." She put her hand on his cheek, wanting to take away all the pain in his eyes. "Am I so pathetic that I need to torment you just so I can feel better?" As she said the words, she felt a rising strength within her, a self-confidence she hadn't felt in a very long time, if ever. "I know how you feel about me. I don't need a secret to believe in you." And she knew she was right. Steen was who he was, and she believed in him. "You don't ask me to be who I'm not, so I'm not going to ask you to betray yourself."

His eyes narrowed. "You're leaving, aren't you? You're not staying tonight."

"I'm leaving in ten days."

"I meant with me. You're not staying with me, tonight. That's why you're letting me off the hook. Because you've already walked away emotionally."

"Steen—"

"I was in prison, Erin. I was in prison for four years."

Her stomach dropped and her blood ran cold. "What?"

"The day I ran into you when your car broke down, Chase had just picked me up from prison." He gestured at the blue sky. "I haven't seen the sky in four years. I hadn't been able to make my own choice about where I go, what I eat, or when I sleep for four years. I'm on parole. I'm still not free. I can't leave the state. I have to get a job and report in, like a fucking kid who might get in trouble if he's not kept busy." His eyes were blazing. "I'm an ex-con, Erin, and I always will be."

She felt like she was going to throw up. Steen had been in prison? "For what? Why were you in there?" There had to be an explanation. Something that made sense.

"Attempted murder."

※ ※ ※

Steen steeled himself as he watched Erin's face blanch in response to his undiplomatic announcement. She looked like she was going to pass out. Shit. He really wished he'd learned tact at some point in his life.

"Attempted murder?" she echoed, her voice faint. "Who?"

He gritted his teeth, but he was committed now. "You remember Rachel?" God, he hated to say the words. He hated to relive that moment. But it would haunt him forever. He'd relived it every day for the last four years. Saying it aloud wouldn't bring back the memories. The memories were always there, at the front of his mind. But saying it aloud would reveal it to Erin, and that…shit…that just felt really, really bad.

Her jaw dropped open. "You tried to murder *her*?"

Shocked ripped through him. "Shit, no. Is that what you think of me? You think I'd try to murder a woman?"

Her eyes widened. "No, of course not, but you just said—"

"Her husband," he clarified. This was unraveling fast. Shit. He had no idea how to handle this. "You remember when

I said that her husband caught us?"

She nodded mutely, her eyes wide.

"Well, when he walked into the hotel room and found us together, he was pissed, drunk, and carrying a knife." Hell, he remembered every detail of that night.

Erin's hand went to her heart. "A knife? What kind of knife?"

"The kind you use if you're some commando wannabe who thinks he's a badass." He could still remember the size of the blade as it slashed toward him. He'd never forget the drunken howl of rage as the bastard took a swipe, or the feel of the metal plunging into his shoulder as he ducked. "He went right for my throat. I dodged it, but he hit my shoulder." He instinctively touched the scar, a visceral reminder of how stupid he'd been to trust Rachel when she'd invited him back to her room. He'd been so unaware of what was about to happen, completely clueless that she'd left the door open for the sole reason of getting caught by her husband, just to pay him back for cheating on her. He'd been used, and he'd had no fucking idea until it was too late. "He came after me again, but when I deflected the blow, I knocked him down. His knife hit his neck and sliced *his* jugular." He would never forget the scent of blood, or how bright red it was. There had been so much blood. The screams of Rachel, and the way her husband's breath had started to gurgle—

"Steen." Erin touched his arm, jerking him back to the present. "Are you okay?"

He stared at her hand on his arm. She was touching him. On purpose. Even though she knew what he'd done. He dragged his gaze off her hand and looked at her. "They said I had attacked him. Rachel said I tricked her into letting me into the hotel room, and that I was sexually assaulting her. She claimed her husband heard me in the hall, and he broke in to save his wife. They said it was my knife, and I attacked him without provocation. They both testified that I went to her room to punish her for rejecting me at the bar earlier that evening. It was their testimony that made the jury not believe my self-defense plea. Four years in prison."

And that was it. The truth. The entire, ugly truth.

Erin removed her hand from his. "How did you get

stabbed this last time? That happened in prison, right?"

He frowned, trying to follow her questioning. Why had she changed the subject? Why wasn't she peppering him with questions, challenging his slant of the story? He shrugged noncommittally. "I stepped in front of a knife. Bad timing."

She cocked her head, studying him. "What really happened, Steen?"

He gritted his jaw. "A new kid was targeted. It was his first day, and I knew he had no defense. I was getting out soon, and I didn't give a shit if I died. So, I took the hit for him."

Her eyes widened. "You stepped in front of the knife and let the guy stab you?"

He shrugged. "Yeah, well, someone had to help the kid."

"No, no one had to. You just did." She took a breath, and let it out. "Okay."

He frowned. "Okay, what?"

"I'll stay with you tonight."

It took a full minute for her words to register. "What?"

She managed a half-smile, though her eyes were still wary. "I believe it was self-defense with Rachel's husband, Steen. I was on the receiving end of her barbs enough times to know she very well could be the kind of person to lie on a witness stand to exonerate herself, so the conviction means nothing to me. I believe *you*. I'm so incredibly sorry that she betrayed you like that, and then left you to rot in prison. It's not fair. It's wrong. I know nothing I say can change the fact you had to endure it, but it's still wrong."

He felt something tighten in his chest, and for a minute, he had trouble breathing. There was no acrimony or judgement in her words, and her hand was still on his arm. She knew he was an ex-con, imprisoned for attempted murder, and *she was still touching him.* "You don't care?"

"Of course I care." She moved her horse closer. "I am so sorry that you endured that. And I'm so sorry you almost died. But I'm so glad that you were able to save the life of that man, whose family is probably very happy they didn't get a phone call that someone they loved died that day. Maybe you were meant to be there. Maybe you had to be in prison because he had to be saved. He's a good guy, isn't he? The man you saved?"

Somehow, it didn't surprise him that Erin would assume a prison inmate might be a "good guy." And she was right. "Yeah, he is." He thought of the kid's dad. "His family was glad he was okay," he admitted, mulling over her words. He'd never thought of it that way. He'd never considered the fact that Pointer would be dead now if he hadn't been in prison. It was weird to consider that, although he didn't exactly buy into the fact that he had been destined to save him all along.

Erin smiled then, and wrapped her arms around his neck. "I believe in you, Steen. Build your house here. Make a home. You deserve it."

Build your house here. God, the words were too much. She actually believed he belonged here, that he deserved to call this place home. "Erin." Her name was a throaty whisper as he wrapped his arm around her waist and dragged her off her horse onto his lap. She snuggled into him immediately. Her body was soft and warm against his, and she felt so damn right in his arms. "You have to go home," he said, even as he threaded his fingers through her hair, pressing his face into the curve of her shoulder, inhaling the scent he would always associate with her: that delicate flowery scent that was too elusive to identify. "You would never fit in here."

She lifted her face to his. "I'm a vet, Steen. I do animals. Isn't a ranch exactly where I might fit?"

Something seemed to stick in his chest, a memory of so long ago when his mother had made a promise to always be there, and then she'd disappeared. A familiar shield tightened around his chest. "Don't make promises, Erin. We both know we're a couple of broken people right now, and we're helping each other. But that's short term. When you heal, and you realize how amazing you are, life with an ex-con isn't going to sound so good."

Her brow furrowed. "Steen—"

"No." He put his finger over her lips. "Don't make any promises." He'd believed in Rachel when they were in high school, and he'd sure as hell believed in her when he'd run into her five years ago. He didn't want promises from Erin, because they hurt when they were broken. Erin wouldn't mean to break her promise, but she would, because there was no way she would be able to live his life, with the stigma he'd carry forever. "Just make it about today. That's all I want."

She studied him for a long moment, then nodded. "Okay. Today then." She draped her arms around his neck. "I have to go get my stuff. I'll be back early evening. Sound good?"

Good? A warmth began to spread through him, a deep satisfaction he hadn't felt in a very long time. "Yeah. It does." He kissed her again, not a long one, just enough to make a statement.

A statement that he was going to keep her, for as long as she was willing to stay.

And then, he was going to let her go, even if it was the most difficult thing he'd ever done in his life.

Chapter 13

"We're going on a date."

At Steen's announcement, Erin looked up from filing the last notes from the day's patients in Josie's antiquated filing cabinets. There were no electronic files here, which Erin actually found sort of refreshing. She was so accustomed to a life of gleaming medical equipment and patients worth hundreds of thousands of dollars. It was such a shift to be dealing with animals who simply lived with the people who owned them, animals who mattered for reasons other than as a million dollar investment. She'd spent the morning driving to assorted ranches, and the afternoon had been spent in office hours. She'd seen three large mixed-breed dogs, a Chihuahua, a gecko, and sixteen cats, the latter of which had all been owned by the same woman. She was really hoping the cat lady wasn't a warning from the universe about what her future held now that she was divorced and hopelessly infatuated with a man who had absolutely zero interest in pursuing anything long term.

She and Steen had talked deeply over the last few days about his past and hers, but he'd continuously made it apparent that he believed their time together had to end when her stint as Josie's replacement was over. He'd erected a wall between them that she couldn't break through. She was incredibly frustrated with him. Why did she think she cared that he had been in prison? He was innocent, and she didn't need a pardon from the governor to know that.

But Steen was stubborn, and twice he'd actually walked

out when she'd pushed too hard.

But now, he was here, at her office, looking like a civilized, incredibly handsome fantasy man as he lounged in the doorway of the clinic's business office. He was still wearing his battered cowboy hat, but his dark blue jeans looked brand new, as did his blue plaid shirt that made his eyes vibrant. Even his well-creased cowboy boots had clearly been polished up for the night. His jeans were low on his hips, showcasing his lean physique and his broad shoulders. He was almost clean-shaven, with a hint of whiskered shadow on his face, as if he couldn't quite eliminate it. In the short time since she'd reconnected with him, he'd already put on weight, and his stamina had improved. He was healing quickly, and he no longer looked like a man who'd almost died recently. He looked, in fact, like a dangerous predator ready to eat her up...which was a really, really tantalizing thought. She couldn't keep the anticipation from fluttering through her as she watched him lounge against the doorframe, looking so deliciously masculine that she was pretty sure he would be illegal in certain states.

Yes, indeed, there was nothing weak about him anymore. He'd been putting on serious muscle, which she knew from the last few nights in his bed, learning exactly how amazing it was to be truly desired by a man. The fact that Steen was tireless in his dedication to finding out exactly what she liked and what she didn't had made for some very late nights and some incredible discoveries.

It had been the best days of her life...and she was all too aware the clock was ticking. There were only six days left until she had to leave. Six days until he would gently, but firmly, kick her out the door and back to her life.

Her throat constricted, but she lifted her chin. No. She wasn't going to think about that.

If he could keep his distance, then so could she. She leaned back in her chair and laced her fingers through her hair. "Maybe I don't want to go on a date with you. Did you think of asking, instead of demanding?"

"I considered it, but I didn't want to give you the opportunity to say no." He produced a bouquet of roses from behind his back and held them out. "For you."

She stared at the flowers, too surprised to react. "No one has ever brought me flowers before." Damn him. The moment she resolved to pull back from him, he had to give her *flowers*. With a resigned sigh, she shook her head, knowing full well that if six more days were all she could have with him, then she'd take those six days and imprint every last second in her memory.

"Then you, my dear, have led a deprived life in which you've been surrounded by idiots." He levered himself off the doorframe and strode across the small office toward her. She couldn't help the shiver of anticipation as he walked around the desk toward her. He plucked the pen out of her hand, clasped her wrist, and pulled her to her feet with just enough force to send her tumbling against his chest.

Then he wrapped his arm around her waist, locking her against him, and kissed her. She should have been accustomed to being kissed by him, but even after several days of constant attention, she still felt her heart leap every time his mouth descended upon hers. Sometimes his kiss was gentle. Sometimes it was demanding and rough. Sometimes it was flirty and mischievous. And other times, like this, it was a sensual kiss that promised an eternity.

This was her favorite kiss.

With a sigh of pure contentment, she draped her arms around his neck and leaned into him, kissing him back, thoroughly enjoying the prickle of his whiskers against her face, and the feel of his lips against hers. He was pure, dangerous seduction, and she'd never felt so alive.

Just as the kiss began to change into something that was going to lead to naked-office-time, he pulled back, but he didn't release her. "That's for later. Right now, I want to take you out."

She lightly grasped the front of his shirt and tugged him gently. "You don't need to court me, Steen. I know you don't have any money, and I'm a sure thing tonight anyway."

Darkness flickered in his eyes, but it wasn't seduction. It was anger, and she realized she shouldn't have mentioned the money. "I can afford to take you to dinner," he said, his voice on edge. "I'm not that pathetic."

"I didn't mean—"

He shoved the flowers in her hand. "I'll be outside

if you want to come. If you don't, that's fine." He turned and walked out without another word, leaving her holding the most beautiful flowers she'd ever received…well, the only flowers she'd ever received from a man, standing there in her dirty jeans, muddy hiking boots, and "didn't bother to shower this morning" hair.

She should have known better than to bring up the finances. No man wanted to feel like he couldn't support a woman. Dammit. Frustrated, she grabbed her purse and followed him out of the building.

He was leaning against the front fender of one of the ranch's pickup trucks, his arms folded over his chest. His hat was tipped low over his forehead, but she felt his gaze the moment she stepped outside.

After locking the door, she walked over to him and stopped just in front of him.

He didn't move.

She sighed and flicked his hat back so she could see his face. "Stop it."

He narrowed his eyes. "Stop what?"

"Being a shit."

His eyebrows nearly shot off his forehead. "Did you just swear at me? You never curse."

"I reserve them for appropriate moments, like this one." She set her hands on her hips. "Listen, Steen. I get that you have baggage. Between your mom ditching you, your loser dad, and your lack of bond with your brothers, I understand you have no comprehension of how much you have to offer. I realize the impact that a prison record could have on your future. I understand all that, but I'll be honest, at some point, you have to get over it. Move on." She held out her arms and gestured at herself. "Look at what's right in front of you, and appreciate it, because before you know it, it will be gone."

He stared at her for a long moment, and then sighed. "I'm sorry."

"For what?"

"For being a shit." The corner of his mouth quirked. "You're right. I know you better than that, and I know that you didn't mean it as an insult when you questioned my ability to pay for dinner. Just because I expect to be judged by people in general doesn't make it fair that I reacted that way to you." He held out his hand. "May I have a second chance, fair maiden? I'd like to take you out on the town tonight, on my dime, of which I am sure I can scrape up a sufficient number to pay for dinner, and I promise I won't take offense at any prison jokes you might make. Deal?"

Her irritation fled, and she shook his hand. "Deal."

He grinned. "Then we have a date."

A date. Her first official date with Steen, more than a decade since she'd first seen him.

Hot damn.

❦ ❦ ❦

Steen really didn't care about the menu. He'd barely glanced at the wine list before ordering one. And he hadn't even bothered to try the bread that the waiter had left on the table.

It was all about Erin tonight. That was it. Just Erin. She was the only thing he wanted to notice, the only thing he *could* notice. She simply outshone every other damn thing in existence.

Her eyes were sparkling, and she was sexy as hell in her jeans and tee shirt. She'd complained about going to dinner in her work clothes, but he hadn't let her go home to change. He preferred her this way: natural, casual, and happy. Plus, he'd been half-afraid she'd change her mind about going out if she got home. Another part of him had also been concerned that she might put on some fancy outfit for dinner, reminding them both that she was out of his league. As a rural vet in her jeans and tee shirt, she was accessible, vulnerable, and reachable. She was a real person, and he was able to simply be with *her*. She knew, however, that simple and casual weren't her real life, and if she got dressed up, it would be a constant reminder that she belonged somewhere else. Yeah, he knew she did, but tonight, he wanted it to be just about them. Besides, he liked her this way. He'd told her she looked beautiful exactly as she was and he'd meant every word of it.

The last four days of making love to her in his

bunkhouse every night had been incredible. He couldn't believe how responsive she was to him, how completely she trusted him. It was surreal and amazing. He knew that this time with her would somehow sustain him for the rest of his life when the reality of his existence descended after her departure.

He knew she would have been perfectly fine with another night over the grill behind the bunkhouse, but he wanted more for her. He wanted her to know what it felt like to be taken out for a nice dinner. He wanted her to know that he was proud to be with her. It was important to him that she understand that, so he'd made the decision to venture out into town for the first time since his release from prison.

He'd chosen a classy restaurant in the adjoining town, hoping that he wouldn't run into anyone who would know him and where he'd been for four years. In the town where he'd once been a superstar, the big man on campus, he now wanted nothing more than to be anonymous, so he could treat Erin to the night she deserved. He wanted her to enjoy herself, not be burdened by the history of the man she was with.

Steen was aware the place wasn't as fancy as she was used to, but it was about as high class as he was going to find in the area. The wine glasses looked appropriately sparkly. He figured the white tablecloths were up to standard, and even he had to admit the candlelight was romantic. He didn't consider himself a romantic. As a general rule, he saw candles as potential fire hazards and a waste of a good flame, but for the first time in his life, they made him think of the softness of her skin, and the way her hair felt beneath his fingers.

Erin leaned back in her chair, surveying the small restaurant. "It's amazing. Thank you."

He shrugged as the waiter approached with their wine. "It's what you deserve. I want you to know that I'm proud to be with you."

She grinned at him, and leaned forward, her fingers brushing against his in a public display of affection that made something inside him shift. She wasn't afraid to acknowledge she was with him. He'd half-thought she wouldn't want to be seen in public with an ex-con, but not only had she agreed to come to dinner, but she was *touching* him. The thought shook him to his core as he looked down at her fingers tapping the back of his hand.

"Thank you," she said. "I'm having a great time."

He considered moving his hand away for her own protection, but he couldn't make himself do it. Instead, he flipped his hand over and wrapped his fingers around hers. "You're welcome." He grinned at her, and she smiled back, an intimate exchange that was only about them, and their connection. He leaned forward, lowering his voice. "Erin—"

"Steen Stockton? Is that you?"

Steen's entire body tensed as his name was called from across the room, and he quickly pulled his hand away from Erin's. He saw the look of surprise on her face, but he didn't have time to apologize as he turned toward the door. When he saw the man striding toward him, his gut dropped down to his boots. Shit. He was sunk.

Swearing under his breath, he rose to his feet and shook hands with Walt Parker, one of the Rogue Valley High School alums who had funded much of the football team's expenses when Steen had been playing for them. He knew Walt well, or he had, back before his life had imploded.

Walt thudded his hand on Steen's shoulder, then pulled back to inspect him. The older man's face was leathery from years in the sun, but he was as fit and lean as ever, easily recognizable as the man who'd held the passing record at the school for a decade until Steen had broken it. "Good to see you, Steen. It's been too long."

Steen glanced at Erin, who was watching with interest. "Um, yeah, I've been busy." He wasn't sure whether Walt knew what had happened with Rachel. God help him, he didn't want Erin to endure the stigma he'd carry for the rest of his life.

"You come by to see the display, in honor of the school's fiftieth anniversary?" Walt asked.

Steen frowned. "What display?"

"You didn't recognize the table by the front door when you came in? Or the chair you're sitting in?" Walt's eyebrows shot up. "Or the buffet where the wine display is set up?"

Steen's gaze shot to the chair that his hand was still on. He recognized the design immediately. He glanced at the wine display, and remembered all too well the hours he'd spent in that crappy basement carving the table by hand. It looked good, weathered properly. Behind him, was the dining room table he'd made to seat all his brothers after their dad had busted up their table in one of his rages. All his work, furniture he'd labored over as a teenager, back when spending hours building furniture had been his only respite from the life that stalked him. "Where did you get those?"

"Your stuff is all over the area. I buy 'em up when I see 'em." He grinned. "I have to support my fellow ball players, right, my man?" He pointed to a painting by the front door. "That's from Don Simms, a wide receiver who was a few years ahead of you." He winked. "Between you and me, he wasn't all that talented, but he's one of us, so his stuff hangs."

Steen frowned, still trying to process what he'd inadvertently stumbled into, an apparent shrine to his high school football team. "You own this place? What about the winery you were running?"

"I still own it, but I decided I wanted to teach people about the beauty of pairing fine wine with good food." Walt grinned. "Tonight's dinner is on me." He bowed at Erin. "Any woman accompanying a former RVHS football player dines on the house. Welcome, my dear. My treat tonight." He shook Steen's hand again and then headed off to another table, waxing poetically about the wine.

Steen sat back down to find Erin staring at him. "You build furniture?"

"I used to. I built furniture for my mom and me because we couldn't afford to buy it. I liked doing it, and so I built some stuff to sell." He scowled, staring at his wine, irritated that he'd managed to choose the only restaurant in the area where he would know the damned owner. At the same time, he felt an immense sense of relief that his past hadn't come up, though now that he'd been identified, it was possible that his veil of invisibility could slide off at any moment. "Once my mom left me with my dad, I kept building stuff, trying to save enough money so when she came back for me, I could take care of her. In the end, the old man found my stash of cash when I was at a game and he used it on a prostitute—"

He paused when Erin got up and walked away from the table toward the buffet behind him.

He twisted around to watch as she approached the buffet, tensing as she crouched beside it and ran her hand down the leg. He remembered the mistake he'd made on that one, taking a divot out of the inside. It figured that would be the one she'd choose to inspect.

She spent several minutes at the buffet, then walked over to the table by the door. Steen shifted restlessly, uncomfortably with her close inspections, but at the same time, he was sort of... well...he wasn't sure what he thought of her interest.

After a few minutes, she came and sat back down across from him. She folded her arms over her chest and studied him.

He waited.

She didn't say anything.

Finally, he couldn't stand it anymore. "Well?"

"You have a gift."

Stupidly, he felt like grinning. He knew that the furniture was decent. It was the only thing besides football and horses that he was any good at, and her response felt really good. But he simply shrugged, pretending it wasn't a big deal. "It's been a long time."

"It's not furniture. It's art." She leaned forward. "What other art have you done?"

He shifted. "Nothing."

"Do you draw? Paint? Make mosaics out of horse manure?"

He grinned that time. "No, just the furniture, but if I can't find a job, I'll be sure and consider the horse manure as a possible career choice."

She didn't smile. "I'm serious, Steen. Do you like making furniture?"

He shrugged again. "I don't know. I just did it. Like I said, it's been a long time." He picked up his glass, letting the red wine glisten beneath the dim lights. "Tonight is about you, not furniture. I raise my glass to the most incredible woman I've ever met in my life, whose soul lights my way and has since the day I first saw her."

Erin's face softened, and she smiled. "That's beautiful.

Thank you." She grinned at him, her eyes teasing. "But I know you're avoiding the topic. Why don't you want to talk about the furniture?"

He put the glass down. "Because it's from a long time ago. I can't make a living at it, and I can't take it with me when I move on."

"Move on?" She frowned. "To where? You've decided not to stay at the ranch?"

"I don't belong there. I never did."

She leaned forward. "Do you *want* to stay?"

He met her gaze, and suddenly, he wanted to say yes. He wanted to stay with her on that damned ranch and do nothing else but lose himself in her for the rest of his life. But that wasn't reality. Making love to her all day wouldn't feed them or give them a life. And he wasn't going to live off the pity of half-brothers who didn't need his shit. "I need to go. I don't belong there."

When she opened her mouth to protest, he put his hand over hers. "I don't want to talk about it, Erin. I just want this to be about you."

She wrinkled her nose at him. "You're being a toad."

He grinned. "A toad? Really? How's that?"

"I'm a woman. I don't like to be ignored when I have something to say."

He sighed and leaned back in his seat. The last thing he wanted to do was disempower her. Shit. He didn't know how to do this supportive guy thing. "Okay, talk."

Her faced softened. "Really?"

The vulnerability in her expression severed the last bit of resistance he had. He leaned forward, lowering his voice. "Erin, listen to me. Yeah, I don't want to talk about my relationship with my half-brothers, or my life. I'm a mess. I get that. There's no way to fix it or to change what my life has been, or to erase all the black marks on my past. I think you're the kindest, most optimistic woman on the face of the planet because you actually care enough to want to fix it. It matters to me what you think. If you have something you want to say, then I'll sit here and listen to every word until you're finished."

She studied him for a long moment. "You don't have to

be defined by your past," she finally said.

He sighed, realizing she wasn't going to take his thinly veiled suggestion to talk about sunsets and nakedness instead of his life. "I agree. It doesn't define me, but at the same time, it's a part of who I am."

She cocked her head, studying him. "You don't want to be here, do you?"

He frowned. "Of course I do. I want to take you to a nice dinner."

"But not here." She gestured at the tablecloth. "This isn't your kind of place, is it?"

Well, there was no way to deny that truth, so he shrugged one shoulder. "I wanted to do something nice for you."

"Which I appreciate very much." She reached across the table and took his hand. "Here's the thing, Steen. I haven't thought of you every day for the last decade because you're the kind of guy who will take me out for dinner at a restaurant with linen napkins. The man who matters to me is the one who grew up dirt poor and came to school with holes in his jeans. He's the one who was willing to fight the bullies and get black eyes if he had to. The man who would work all day under the broiling sun to help a horse." She leaned forward. "I came back here to get away from white tablecloths, Steen. That's not what I want. I want *you*, exactly the way you are. So, if tonight was about you, where would we be eating? Where would the real Steen choose for his first night out in four years?"

Heat seemed to pour through him at her words. For a moment, he could only stare at her as her words tumbled through him, igniting a fire that seemed to burn right through his belly. She was absolutely right. He didn't want to be here. He wanted to be somewhere where the very pulse of life beat through him and called to him. For four years, he'd lived in a world that left his soul silent and empty. He didn't want to be there anymore. He wanted to be alive.

Silently, he tossed cash on the table to pay for their untouched wine, stood up, and held out his hand to her.

Her face lit up, and she put her hand into his. "Where are we off to, cowboy?"

He locked his arm around her back and dragged her up

against him. He knew it wasn't proper, but in that moment, he didn't give a damn. He kissed her anyway, hot, wet, and with all the raging passion she'd just unleashed inside him. She melted into his body, kissing him back with every bit of the same need that he'd poured into her.

Swearing, he broke the kiss. "I want to rip your clothes off," he whispered. "But first, I want to take you somewhere."

She smiled. "It's about time."

Chapter 14

Erin felt her entire body relax when she walked into the Saddle Rack Tavern with Steen. The crowded bar was low lit, with unfinished wood beams, chandeliers made of battered wagon wheels, and tables that looked like they'd been recycled from old barns. There was a band on the low corner stage, four twenty-something guys in cowboy hats and blue jeans, winking at the audience with such charm she almost wanted to swoon herself.

The place was rowdy with the rumble of good-natured conversation. Almost every man had a cowboy hat on, and Wranglers were on just about every person she saw. The women came in all types: some who looked like they could wrangle a steer as well as any man, but there were also ones who weren't afraid to show they were a woman who could clean up just fine. There wasn't a single suit in sight, and no diamond earring studs flashing in the dim lighting.

It was real, without airs, and it felt like the home she'd never had.

She slid her hand into Steen's and leaned against his arm. "It's perfect."

He grinned down at her, a smile so genuine and full that she felt her heart flutter. Despite all the time she'd spent with him over the last few days, she'd always felt a sense of distance from him. It had felt as if he'd been holding back, and now that she saw the light dancing in his eyes, she realized she'd been right.

She hadn't seen the real Steen until now. Well, she's seen parts of his true self, but he'd been guarded, unwilling to let her truly see who he was. Right now, though, he looked...happy. Comfortable. Like he belonged. "It's been a long time since I've been here," he said, his dark eyes sparkling. "Any interest in a quick spin on the dance floor before we eat?"

"Dance?" She hadn't danced in years. The thought of having Steen's strong arms wrapped around her on the dance floor made excitement rush through her. How awesome did that sound? There was something so magical about being held in a man's arms while the music wove through her soul. "I'd love to dance. Really?"

"You bet." He led the way through the crowd, threading easily across the room to a dark corner of the sparsely populated dance floor. There were hardly any people dancing, but Steen didn't appear to care. The moment they reached the spot he'd apparently wanted, he turned toward her and pulled her into his arms.

The song was upbeat with a contagious rhythm, but Steen locked her against him anyway. He put one hand on her lower back, took her hand, and then began to move her around the dance floor. His dancing was effortless, in perfect time to the beat, and he moved his hips like he was made for music, sweeping her with him. He grinned at her as he spun her around, keeping her so tight against him it was as if they were moving as a single unit. Laughter bubbled up through her as they danced. The music seemed to come alive inside her, and her heart felt lighter than it ever had.

"God, you're gorgeous." He pulled her closer, so close that their knees bumped. He immediately slid his knee between hers, and suddenly, they were moving even more tightly together, their bodies moving in perfect unison, threaded together from shoulder to knee. He directed her with both the pressure of his hand on her lower back, and the unspoken commands of his body, turning her with his hips, his shoulders, and his torso.

She realized he was singing to her as they danced, the words to the song whispered in her ear in perfect tune as he whirled her around. His voice was beautiful, so melodic and deep she knew he could easily be on stage instead of on the dance floor. Music flowed through him as if it were a part of him, and he brought her into that magical circle, moving her with such indefinable grace and musicality that she felt as if she were being whirled around by a breeze on a perfect spring day.

Except it wasn't a breeze. It was the raw, untamed strength of his body that was moving her, and she was locked against him by his hand on her back, and the angle he was holding her. He was leaning forward slightly, using his body as a shield to tuck her against him. She felt as though she were completely protected from everything, cradled by the strength of his presence while still being swept away by the grace of his dancing.

She was so aware of every place their bodies touched. Her skin seemed to tingle everywhere, and she wanted to laugh aloud with happiness. She'd never felt so free, so adored, or so graceful.

The song ended, but he didn't even hesitate, never breaking stride as he merged their dance into the next song, effortlessly adjusting their steps to the new beat. She was astounded by what a wonderful dancer he was, so hopelessly out of her class.

"Just let me lead you," he whispered to her, his voice so deep and sexy that heat seemed to ignite deep in her belly. "Feel the music in your soul and let it fill you. Feel my body against yours, and let yourself connect with me. Follow me, sweetheart. I won't let you fall." He pressed a kiss to her earlobe, still keeping her tucked up against him as he spun them across the floor. "Just feel my soul touching yours, and you'll be with me."

Her throat constricted with sudden emotion, but she closed her eyes, focusing her entire being on Steen. She felt the heat of his body through her clothes, and the sheer hardness of his frame against her. Yet, at the same time, she became aware of the fluidity of his hips, moving against hers. She focused on the movement of his body, softening her muscles, relaxing into him. The moment she did so, she felt herself melt into him, and suddenly, she was completely in sync with him.

Her body seemed to know exactly what Steen wanted from her, and it became effortless to move in unison with him. Her thigh was between his, but she never tripped over his feet or even moved the opposite way of him. The dance became true beauty, filling her with the sheer presence of Steen, and the magic of the music uplifting her.

"You've got it," Steen whispered against her ear as they whirled across the floor. "We're completely connected. God, you're hot. I could dance with you every second for the rest of my life, and it still wouldn't be enough."

Sheer delight bubbled up through her. "You're an incredible dancer."

"Inspired by you," he replied, pressing a kiss to the side of her neck without losing the beat. "I only dance when I'm at peace inside, otherwise I can't feel the music at all. You need to have a completely quiet soul to hear the music. It's like working with troubled horses. The magic happens in the inner silence of the soul."

His words were so heartfelt, she felt her throat tighten. This was the man who thought he wasn't good enough for his brothers? Or to take his place in his family? God, he was beautiful, and not just his face. His soul was pure and beautiful, just as she'd always known. She knew she was catching a precious glimpse that he never shared, an inside peek at the man he tried so hard to hide.

Instinctively, she tightened her grip on his shoulder. "That was beautiful," she said. "Kiss me."

He lifted his head from where he'd had it tucked against the side of hers. His eyes were dark and beautiful, peaceful for the first time she could remember. He searched her face for a moment, and then he kissed her.

The kiss was different than it had ever been before. It was sensual and demanding, as always, but this time, there was something else. An emotion. A need. A connection. She realized it was the first time Steen had kissed her with all of himself, instead of holding back and giving her only the part of himself he was willing to give.

There was a tenderness to his kiss now. A softness. A realness. It was a kiss that touched her heart in a way that it had never been touched.

Steen cradled her face as he kissed her, his touch so gentle she felt as though she could be made of the most fragile china and she would still be safe in his arms. She wrapped her fingers around his wrists, kissing him back until she felt like her heart was going to explode.

It wasn't until she heard the catcalls and the whistles that she realized the music had stopped.

Heat flooded her cheeks as she pulled back, but Steen didn't let her retreat. He kissed her again, longer, and her heart seemed to soar when she realized he didn't care about the whistles or the attention. He wasn't finished kissing her, and he had no plans to stop until he was done.

With a happy sigh, she melted back into him and enjoyed every last moment of the kiss until he finally pulled back, just enough to break the kiss, but his body was still against hers, and his hands still cradled her face.

He grinned at her, and kissed the tip of her nose. "Hey."

She smiled back. "Hi."

"That was fun."

She giggled at his understatement. "Yes, it was."

"Want to dance again when the band comes back on stage?"

She rolled her eyes. "What do you think?"

He kissed the tip of her nose. "I'll take that as a yes." He kissed her one last time, a deep, delicious kiss of connection, and then swung his arm over her shoulder, tucking her up against him as he escorted her off the dance floor. "This place makes great burgers. You up for that?"

"Of course." It felt so natural to be nestled against him, and she wasn't blind to the appreciative glances of the other women as they walked toward an empty table. She also noticed that Steen didn't even noticed the women gawking at him. He was drop-dead gorgeous, yet he had no awareness of it whatsoever. He was simply watching her. After having her husband leave her for another woman, the fact that Steen was literally unaware of the feminine adoration he was receiving was so amazing.

It was incredible to be the focus of his attention. She was so accustomed to being barely seen, that to have Steen entirely focused on her was almost surreal. It felt incredible. She grinned at him. "You make me feel amazing. Thank you."

"Hey." He paused at an empty table and pulled her against him. "You're the one who deserves the thanks. I forgot what it felt like to be alive. You've changed everything for me."

"Mutual benefit, then." She couldn't keep the smile off her face as he pulled out the chair for her. "Thanks."

"You bet." He eased into the seat adjacent to hers, immediately resting his hand on the back of her chair. There was no doubt about the fact that he was claiming her, and she loved it. He made her feel like she was the most special woman in the entire world, and it felt incredible.

She didn't want to go back home to her life. She wanted to stay with Steen, to feel every moment of the way he made her feel. The depth of her need stunned her, and she realized that if he asked her right now, she would stay.

The realization was shocking, and terrifying. Would she really give up everything she'd worked so hard to achieve for a man who made her feel alive? She had spent her entire life dedicating every last inch of herself to what she'd finally managed to achieve professionally. She'd developed self-worth through her work accomplishments, because she hadn't been able to earn it in her personal life. Steen thought she was a simple vet, but she wasn't. She was a highly specialized equine orthopedic surgeon, specializing in elite, expensive athletes, and she could never do here what she did in her real life. In this area, there weren't many horses of that extreme caliber, the surgery facilities didn't exist, and most potential clients didn't have the money to pay for that kind of work. If she walked away from what she'd accomplished and put herself entirely in the hands of Steen, what would she have left for herself? What would she have to fall back upon when he realized he wanted something else, someone else? Her chest tightened, and suddenly she felt sick to her stomach. Would she really consider giving all that up for him, if he asked? She'd given everything to try to impress her husband and her parents. Was she actually willing to give it all up for another man?

His eyes narrowed. "What?"

She blinked. "What?"

"You were just thinking something serious. I saw it in your eyes. What's up?"

She shook her head, trying to erase the thoughts from

her head. She didn't want to ruin this moment with real life. "Nothing."

He cocked an eyebrow. "Don't lie to me. I know it's not nothing."

She sighed, wrinkling her nose at him in exasperation. "Okay, fine. I was thinking something, but I don't want to tell you."

He eyed her speculatively, and she knew he was considering whether to force it out of her. The last thing she wanted was to talk about how they had no future together, or to even tell him what she'd been thinking. He didn't want a future with her, and to offer him her own future would be against everything she'd worked so hard to achieve.

So, instead, she turned the tables on him. "When you compared dancing to communicating with horses, it made me think about your incredible talent with horses. Don't you have any interest in working with them anymore? You could do that at the ranch." He opened his mouth to protest, and she rushed on. "None of your brothers have your gift. You're the only one who could bring that to the ranch. How can you think you don't add value?"

He said nothing for a long moment, leaning back as a waitress stopped by to take their order. Erin knew he was aware of her attempt to change the subject and he was contemplating whether to let her go ahead with it, or force her back to what he wanted to talk about.

After the waitress was gone, however, Steen answered her question. "Horses aren't my thing anymore."

"Why not?"

"I gave it up to play football."

"But you don't play anymore." She knew she hadn't mistaken the depth of emotion when he'd spoken about the horses. It hadn't been there when he'd talked about the furniture, and it hadn't been there when he'd talked about the football days with Walt, but there had been no mistaking it when he'd mentioned the horses. "Why are you resisting the ranch? Help me understand."

"I quit horses because there was no future. No one respected people who deal with horses. I wanted to get the hell out of my life and be someone, and football was the answer, so that's what I did." Steen let out his breath, looking across the bar. Finally, he looked back at her. "My knee healed after I graduated high school, and I was able to get to college on a full ride. It was my only chance out of my hell. I played three seasons, and then I blew out my knee again, this time for good. I had put everything into football, and I had no backup plan. So, I started riding dirt bikes. It was a rush of adrenaline, a way to outrun the reality of my life, like the fact that my job was pumping gas in a crappy station that was so filthy that even the cockroaches wouldn't rob it."

Erin leaned forward, listening intently. "Did you race the dirt bikes?"

"Yeah. I crashed. I severed my spine." His voice was neutral, but she felt the sudden withdrawal of his energy, as if he were battling memories he didn't want to deal with. "The doctors told me I'd never walk again. They said I was paralyzed for life." He looked at her, and she saw the stark anguish in his eyes. "I was twenty-one years old. The only thing I knew was sports. I had nothing, Erin. Absolutely nothing. It was the scariest moment of my entire life."

Her heart tightened. "But you walk now."

"I fought back with everything I had. I had no insurance to pay for fancy physical therapy. It was all me, and I got my legs working again. I won, and then I lost it all again, and again. Everything I tried, I lost, until I ended up in prison for attempted murder." He leaned forward, his voice low. "But I am scared out of my mind that I'll hurt my back again. If I fall off a horse the wrong way, I'm done. My entire horse career was helping the ones that no one else could handle. I have no interest in shoveling manure for the rest of my life or hauling hay bales around. The only thing I'd want to do on this ranch is deal with the horses that no one else can help, and those are the animals that just might send me back into the worst hell you can ever imagine."

She understood then. She understood everything that drove him. He was afraid, the kind of soul-deep terror that could destroy a life forever. She knew, because she'd lived with that every day of her life. Not the fear of being paralyzed, but the fear of never being loved the way she needed to be loved as a human being. Everything she'd ever done had been driven by that fear. She understood what was driving him, and if she were him, she wasn't sure she'd ever get on a horse again either, not at that risk. "You rode with me."

"The horse wasn't a risk. We had a conversation."

She almost smiled at his answer. He had a conversation with the horse? And he was going to walk away from that? "So, you're going to live in fear your whole life, then?"

He met her gaze. "No. I'm going to live with the memory of our time together. That's what's going to carry me."

She suddenly felt tired, like the weight of the world was on her shoulders. "You're an idiot. Why would you do that? You have a family that wants you to be a part of it. Do you know what I'd do if my family wanted me? I'd never leave their side."

Regret flickered over his handsome face. "Shit, Erin, it's not like that. I'm sorry you have a crappy family. But this is different. They aren't my family. Yeah, I'm related to my half-brothers through our dad, but I don't belong. I can't take charity from them and park myself in the middle of the family ranch that Chase is trying to create." He leaned forward. "*I don't belong there.*"

She could tell he meant it, and she didn't know what to say. Maybe he was right. She didn't know. "Come to Virginia," she said suddenly. "Come back with me."

He stared at her, and her invite fell into the heavy silence.

Oh, God. What had she just done?

⚜ ⚜ ⚜

"Move to Virginia?" Steen repeated softly, his voice low with emotion that seemed to thicken the air around them. "With you?"

"Well, I mean, why not? If you're not going to stay here, and then, well, I don't know. We could..." She shrugged, suddenly embarrassed. "I mean, it's not cowboy country or anything, but there are tons of horses. Or you could build furniture. I have a house in the country, and it has a big workshop out back that I've never used." Excitement began to build. "Seriously, why not?"

He didn't take his gaze off her, and his face was utterly expressionless. She couldn't tell what he was thinking, and suddenly she felt horribly vulnerable and exposed. "Never mind," she muttered. "It was just an idea." God, what had she been thinking? Inviting Steen to move in with her?

Steen leaned forward. "Erin."

The urgency of his tone drew her attention to him, and she looked up, her heart skipping a beat with sudden hope. "What?"

"First of all, I'm pretty much overwhelmed you would offer that. It's a huge statement of trust, and I am honored. But there's no way I would ever allow you to support me."

She spun her fork in her fingers, restless and unsettled. "Maybe money isn't what I need from you. Maybe it's something else." She met his gaze. "Like being loved." She held her breath after she said it. Love? Had she really just said love to him?

His eyes darkened, and electricity seemed to leap between them. "Do you love me?" he asked softly.

She bit her lip and shrugged.

He closed his eyes for a long moment, and she thought she saw his hands tremble. Then he took a breath and leaned forward, staring into her eyes. "Look at me, Erin. I want you to really look at me."

She met his gaze, searching the face that was so familiar to her. His hair was slightly longer than it had been, and his face was less gaunt. She knew his lips so intimately, and could easily envision what it felt like to touch his cheeks. He was so human, so strong, and so vulnerable. "I see a man who was dealt a bad hand in life, and somehow, he has emerged with a pure heart and a good soul. That's what I see."

His face softened, and for a moment, he looked ten years younger. The lines on his face seemed to drop away, and the tension he always carried with him vanished. He bent forward and kissed her, a tender beautiful kiss that made her heart soar. He broke the kiss too soon and rested his forehead against hers. "My sweet Erin," he said quietly. "I don't have a job, or any source of income. As I already told you, I can't even leave the state without the permission of my parole officer. I won't be free of those constraints for at least five years. Don't you see that? I'm an ex-con convicted of a serious, serious crime. I have nothing to offer you, sweetheart, nothing that is remotely worthy of you."

She heard the finality of his words, and her heart sank. She pulled back, searching his face. "You know I don't care about you being in prison, right? You know that I see you for who you are?"

"I know you do." He trailed his fingers in her hair. "And I can't even express how much that means to me." He sighed. "I wish life was different, sweetheart. I wish that on the day when you traded your bike, I'd walked up to you and offered to escort you home. If I'd met you back then, before all this shit happened, everything would have been totally different."

She bit her lip, thinking of how close they'd come back then. She'd had no idea he'd been as aware of her as she'd been of him. All it would have taken was a simple hello, one of them being brave enough to close the gap, and their lives would have been completely different. "Is it really too late for us? Really?"

"Erin, I—" His gaze flicked past her shoulder, and he went sheet white for a split second.

She whirled around, searching for what he'd seen. At first, she saw only crowds of people, and then she saw a woman in a bright red sparkly top heading right for them, her gaze boring into Steen with raw hatred. A woman with gorgeous auburn hair, an amazing body, and a face that promised hell. Erin recognized her immediately, despite all the years that had passed since the last time she'd seen her.

It was Rachel, the woman who sent Steen to prison and left him there to rot, and she was heading right for them.

Chapter 15

Steen felt his entire world closing down upon him as he watched Rachel approach. Every muscle in his body tensed, and his lungs felt like a vice was crushing them. He had no time to escape, nowhere to go. All he could do was sit there and watch her bear down on him, his mind racing frantically as he swept the bar, looking for exits, and finding none close enough. Sweat broke out over his brow as the memories came tumbling back of how she'd set him up. She'd tricked him, and he'd paid for it brutally. Was she going to try again?

Erin moved closer to him, jerking his attention off Rachel. *Jesus.* Erin was in the line of fire now. Erin could be a target. No way in hell could he allow that to happen. He surged to his feet, moving in front of Erin to cut off Rachel as she neared the table.

She stopped a few feet from him, her face a cool mask of thinly veiled disgust. "I heard you were out."

He said nothing, every sense on hyperalert, waiting for her to strike. He would never trust her again, never let her get close enough to destroy him, or anyone that mattered to him.

"You have nothing to say to me?" she asked.

He shook his head once. He sensed Erin stand up behind him, and he shifted his position to block her from Rachel's view. She looked past him, however, her eyes narrowing. "You have a new woman already? Didn't you learn anything?"

He ground his jaw, his pulse thundering in his head. Anger surged through him, fury so thick he felt like it was pouring out of his flesh in black, angry waves. "We have nothing to say to each other," he said neutrally. He became aware that the people near them had stopped talking and were watching them. He realized suddenly that the moment he'd walked into the bar, everyone had known who he was. He'd been so caught up in Erin that he hadn't even noticed. *Shit.*

"We *do* have something to say to each other." Rachel moved closer, so close that her breasts were almost touching his chest, so close that he could smell the alcohol on her breath. He wanted to push her away, but he kept his hands hanging loosely by his side, refusing to be goaded into any contact. He didn't step back, however. There was no way he was going to let her force him to retreat. She might have landed him in prison, but she didn't own him, and he was never going to back down from her again.

"You need to leave," he said, still keeping his voice neutral. "You've been drinking. Go sleep it off."

"You bastard." She slapped his face, and he clenched his jaw, refusing to respond. "You broke your stupid knee, leaving me to find another way out of my life. How dare you fail? I invested years in you, and you failed!"

"Leave him alone." Erin suddenly stepped between them, forcing Rachel to take a step back.

Fear tore through Steen, and he clasped Erin's arm, every nerve ending on fire. He wanted to grab and rush her out the back door, getting her away from Rachel before the viper could strike, but he was frozen in terror, afraid to make one move that could get him thrown back in prison. "Don't get involved," he said quietly, for Erin's ears only. "You have no idea what she's capable of."

But Erin didn't move away. Instead, she put her hands on her hips, and glared at the woman trying to burn him. "Rachel, we all know what happened that night in your hotel room," Erin announced, loudly enough for everyone near them to hear her clearly. "Everyone knows Steen is innocent, and that you set him up to mess with your husband. The truth will damn you, and if you ever come near Steen again, I will make sure the truth comes out."

Steen swore under his breath as Rachel's face contorted

with rage. He tightened his grip on Erin's arm, his heart thundering in fear for her safety. He wasn't free to step in and defend her. He was caught, trapped by Rachel's ability to get his ass thrown back in prison. "Get back," he whispered under his breath, pressing his fingers against her arm to pull her back.

She ignored him.

"You bitch," Rachel snapped at Erin. "Don't threaten me. My father is the District Attorney, and he can crush you both. It will take only one phone call from me to land Steen back in prison, so don't mess with me."

Jesus. Steen went cold at the threat, but at the same time, he knew there was no way he could allow Rachel to bring Erin into this situation. Fury roiling through him, he pulled Erin behind him and used his body to shield her. Rage and fear were thundering through him, but he kept his voice calm and his expression stoic as he faced down the woman who'd destroyed him.

"Rachel," he said evenly, using self-discipline he'd never possessed until prison had taught him that it could save his life. "It's over. The courts settled it. Let it go." He didn't want her to notice Erin too closely and figure out who she was. As much as he didn't want to wind up back in prison, he'd do whatever it took to keep Rachel from turning her sights onto Erin. He was well aware that the night Rachel had approached him five years ago that he'd been dancing with another woman, and he'd always wondered if it had been jealousy that had spurred it. If she'd seen the way he'd been all over Erin, she wouldn't stop until she'd plunged her venom deep into both of them. She'd wanted to use Steen as her ticket out of her life, and she needed to punish him for his failure.

Sure enough, her eyes flashed to the woman he was trying to protect as Erin shoved Steen in the shoulder and came to stand next to him again. *Jesus.* Did she have no sense of self-preservation at all?

"Your new girlfriend?" Rachel spat the words with poison that made adrenaline surge through him.

"No." He didn't even look at Erin. "She's not my type, and you know it. Don't waste your time with her."

Rachel's gaze slithered over Erin in her jeans and tee

shirt, and then appeared satisfied. Without another word, she spun on her stiletto heel and marched away, weaving slightly as she made her way across the crowded floor.

Steen glanced around and saw dozens of people watching him with the avid interest of paparazzi salivating for a story. He swore under his breath. Had he really thought there was any way to escape his past? He was a fool, and he'd brought Erin into it now. He didn't even look at her. "Come on. We need to leave." Under normal circumstances, he'd park himself right back at his table and refuse to be driven out, but the circumstances were far from normal. He didn't want to hang around and give Rachel the chance to hatch some plot to take him down again, or worse, hurt Erin. So, he grabbed Erin's purse and handed it to her.

She took it silently, and didn't argue when he put his hand on her lower back and guided her through the crowd that fell silent as they passed. He felt the weight of a thousand eyes on them, and quickly removed his hand from Erin's back, dropping back to several feet behind her as she led the way out of the bar, refusing to mark her as his anymore.

It had been a terrible, selfish mistake to mark Erin as his. He was done lying to himself that he could do this with her. It was over. It *had* to be over. Right now. Forever.

End of story.

※ ※ ※

Steen didn't say a word to Erin once they were in his truck, and she realized almost instantly that he was taking her back toward Josie's house, where she hadn't slept in days. He wasn't taking her back to his bunkhouse.

"This is it, then?" she asked, watching the houses flash by as he headed back into town, where Josie lived in an apartment over her vet clinic. "You're dropping me off, and that's it?"

He didn't look at her. "What if she comes after you?"

Erin bit her lip, gazing out the window. Rachel's hatred had been so evident, and she'd had no mercy about sending Steen to prison for attempted murder four years ago. Erin had never met anyone like that before. Her parents had ignored her, and Louis had withheld any sort of affection and then betrayed her, but she understood now that her traumas in life that she'd struggled so hard to deal with were nothing compared to what Steen had endured.

Prison.

Prison.

A mother who had abandoned him.

An abusive father.

A woman he loved, whose betrayal had been setting him up for attempted murder.

God, how was it possible that his heart was still so pure, and he could still live with such honor? Because she knew that despite all he'd endured, he was the kindest, most honorable human being she'd ever known.

But she could see what his life was. All he had now was a ranch he refused to belong to, and half-brothers he wouldn't accept. She looked over at him as he drove, watching the torment in his handsome features. He was completely alone. It was ugly, his life. It was dirty. It was isolated. It was rough. And it was tainted. She understood now why he would never let her into his life, and why he'd never come to Virginia.

And did she want his life? Did she want to spend her life looking over her shoulder for Rachel to come after him? But even as she thought it, her heart bled for him. He was such a good man, who had spent his life trying to dig out of the quicksand that he'd been born into. He'd survived. He'd defeated it, because he'd stayed a good person, but the external factors would always be there, haunting him, making it impossible for him to ever step out from the shadows.

He silently turned into her driveway and pulled up to the front of the clinic, beside the side door that led to the second floor apartment.

Erin didn't move to get out of the car, and Steen rested his forearms on the steering wheel, staring out the windshield at the darkness. Finally, he shoved open his door, walked around to her side, and pulled hers open. He leaned against the doorframe moodily, his cowboy hat low over his forehead. "You should go," he said softly.

She unfastened her seatbelt and turned sideways in the seat so she was facing him, her feet resting on the running board.

She didn't move to get out, though. The truck was high enough that she was almost at eye-level with him. "I know you think you're worthless," she said quietly, "but you're wrong."

He shook his head. "I don't think I'm worthless. I just know what hand I've been dealt, and how I have to play the cards." He reached for her then, his fingers trailing over the ends of her hair in a touch so gentle that her heart skipped. "I know you're the greatest treasure of my life," he said. "But it's not my right to hold onto you."

Tears filled her eyes and she held out her arms. "Kiss me."

He shook his head. "No. I can't do that to you anymore." His thumb brushed over her lower lip. "It's time, Erin. It's time for you to go back and kick some ass in your life. Find the guy you deserve."

She scooted to the edge of the seat and grabbed the front of his shirt, her fingers digging in when he resisted. "I'm going to go back to Virginia," she said. "But before I do, there's something you need to know."

His jaw flexed, but he still didn't let her pull him toward her. "What's that?"

"I was there tonight, Steen. I saw firsthand what you are going to have to deal with for the rest of your life. I know your past. I know everything about your miserable life and brutal past, and I know that you have blood on your hands, even though it's not your fault. I know every dark secret you have, but I also know your heart." She put her hand on his chest. "I had a crush on you in high school, but not anymore."

He stiffened. "Smart woman."

"I don't have a silly schoolgirl crush anymore," she said, her fingertips digging into his chest. "Because it's all changed for me." She looked at him, barely able to see his eyes in the shadows beneath his hat. "Because now, I see you from the perspective of a woman who doesn't care about hot football players or swagger. I care about the man inside, and it's for that reason, that I have fallen deeply, truly in love with you."

He didn't move.

He didn't even react.

He simply went utterly still, so still that she could hear

every night sound. The hoot of a nearby owl. The sound of a car passing in the distance. But not a word from him.

She tapped his chest lightly. "I know you don't think you're worthy, and you're probably trying to figure out how to make me stop loving you, but you don't get to choose who loves you. Your brothers love you, or at least Chase does. And I love you. You can reject me and your brothers, but that doesn't mean you get to make any of us stop loving you—"

He cut her off with a kiss so deep and passionate that it seemed to merge souls into one. She flung her arms around his neck as he dragged her against him. He grabbed her thighs and wrapped her legs around his hips. She locked herself around him as he carried her across the driveway, one hand on her butt and the other one supporting her back as he kissed her frantically, with a desperation that she could taste in every kiss.

He grabbed the key from its hiding place by the door, and within a split second, he was taking the stairs two at a time, still kissing her relentlessly. He burst into the upstairs hallway, heading unerringly toward the guest bedroom she'd been sleeping in, clearly having taken note of the layout when they'd stopped by several days ago to pick up more of her clothes.

Her heart leapt as he settled her on the bed, dragging off her shirt and bra in a seamless move as he moved over her, using his body to rock her onto her back, breaking the kiss only enough to get his shirt off as well. The moment she felt his bare chest beneath her hands, a part of her soul wanted to cry. Somehow, she knew it would be the last time she'd ever be with him, the last time she'd ever hold this wonderful man in her arms.

"Don't cry, sweetheart." Steen kissed the tears from her cheeks as he framed her face with his hands. "I don't want you to cry."

She clasped his wrists, refusing to let him go. "Sometimes tears are okay, Steen. Sometimes you have to let your heart bleed or you'll never live. I'd rather cry, than to never love enough to feel that kind of pain. I don't want my heart to be hard anymore, no matter how much it hurts to love."

His face softened as he searched her face. "I'm so far from where you are emotionally," he said.

"No, you're not." She managed a smile through her

tears. "You're right here with me, whether you can see it or not." She locked her hands behind his neck. "Make love to me, Steen. Please, make love to me with every last bit of your soul. Just this once, this one time in your life, don't hold anything back from me. That's the gift you can give me."

For a moment, he said nothing, searching her face so intently she felt like he was trying to discern every last scar on her soul and heal every last one by the sheer force of his will. Then, he kissed her, a kiss that was so achingly, mournfully beautiful that she felt as if the lonesome, haunting howl of the wolf had come alive in the kiss.

He broke the kiss and rolled off her, standing beside the bed as he kicked off his boots and shed his jeans and boxer briefs. He didn't let her take hers off, instead sliding them off her body in the most sensual and tender seduction, showering her body with kisses as he exposed her skin.

By the time he'd finally removed the last pieces of her clothing, her body was aching and restless for more. He moved over her, kissing his way up her body before he settled his weight on her. His skin was hot against hers, his body like steel cords of muscle, his kiss the most beautiful seduction. His fingers slid through her hair, caressing her with soulful tenderness.

She wrapped her legs around his hips, her body tightening as his hips moved against hers, his cock sliding over her wetness in a tease that was almost more than she could endure. "Make love to me," she whispered against his mouth. "I want us to be connected forever."

He said nothing, but suddenly everything shifted from sweet seduction to carnal possession and need. It became about lips and tongues, touching and need. It became a desperate attempt for both of them to unleash every last bit of their souls into each other, enough to sustain them forever. His teeth grazed over her nipple, making her body clench. She loved every touch, every kiss, every intimacy. She knew he would never let himself love her, or at least admit it even to himself, but that this moment, the kisses, and the touches, were the words and the emotions he'd never share or acknowledge.

Each kiss was a whisper of his love, of his heart, of his soul, offered to her and no one else, and she treasured every one of them. Louis had said he loved her, but he'd never made her feel loved. Steen had never said he loved her, but she knew she'd never feel as loved as she was in this moment.

His fingers slipped inside her, and she gasped at the invasion, her body begging for more. She was ready for him, so completely, and he knew it. She didn't want any more foreplay. She wanted him inside her. She wanted him to be with her the way that it would never be with anyone else.

As if sensing her need, Steen shifted his position so his cock was pressing against her. Excitement raced through her as she locked her legs around his hips, trapping him. He moved his hips slightly, teasing her, nudging at her entrance.

She couldn't help the groan that escaped her, and he grinned as he caught it in a searing kiss, even as he slid a tiny bit deeper. "You want me?" he whispered.

"God, yes." She gripped his shoulders, shifting restlessly beneath him. "I will always want you, Steen. Just you. No one else." She opened her eyes and stared into his face. She saw the vulnerability in his eyes, and she knew what he needed to hear. Her big, strong man who had survived hell to be here with her needed to hear her say it, despite all his claims to the contrary. "I love you, Steen. With all my heart."

Relief flooded his features, and he thrust deep, plunging into her. He gripped her hair almost desperately, searching her face. "You really love me, don't you?"

"I do." She smiled, even as her body clenched in response to another thrust. "For always."

"You're so incredible." There was a sadness to his words, but he kissed her before she could say anything. From that moment on, there were no more words. Just Steen showing her with his body, his touch, and his kisses how he felt about her. She heard his unspoken words, and she accepted what he offered, the emotions spiraling around them in a rising intensity as the lovemaking became more frantic, until all that was left was the two of them and a need so great that she knew they would never outrun it.

He thrust one final time, and the orgasm flooded her, a magnificent explosion of fireworks that filled her soul with more love than she ever thought possible.

"God, Erin," Steen whispered as the orgasm took him as well. "You're my everything."

It was all he said, the only words he uttered until she fell asleep in his arms, but it was enough.

Chapter 16

"You sure you don't want me to come in?" Steen reached into the bed of his truck and pulled out Erin's two powder blue suitcases. The airport was bustling and busy, with the energy of a place on the move.

She shook her head, her chin held high. She was still wearing jeans, but her shirt was dressier than she'd been wearing in Wyoming, and she was wearing low heels and makeup. Still the Erin he knew, but with hints of the Erin she really was: independent, successful, and on her way back to the life she deserved. "Nope," she said. "I can handle my bags. They aren't heavy."

"I know you can handle them. I just thought..." Shit. He thought what? That he could follow her into the airport and something would change? Something that would make it so he didn't have to stand back and let her walk out of his life? He'd been so certain that letting her go was the right thing to do, but now that he was standing beside her at the curb at the airport, his instincts were screaming at him to stop being an ass and to claim her right then, right there, for all time.

He hadn't seen her for the last several days, since they'd made love after their date. He hadn't planned to drive her to the airport, but this morning, he'd decided he had to see her again, so he'd driven to the clinic to pick her up for the airport.

He hadn't called ahead. He hadn't asked permission. He'd simply waited outside for two hours until she'd finally emerged, with her suitcases in hand. For a long moment, she'd stared at him, and he'd thought that she wasn't going to let him drive her, then she'd handed him her bags and climbed into the cab of his truck.

The relief he'd felt when she'd accepted his offer of a ride had been almost overwhelming, but it had quickly dissipated when awkwardness had arisen between them. On the entire drive to the airport, there had been only casual, meaningless conversation. He didn't know what he'd wanted to say, or how he'd wanted his last moments with her to be, but he knew it wasn't a car ride filled with empty dialogue.

And now, his time was almost out.

He tipped his cowboy hat back on his head, restless and unsettled, searching for answers he couldn't find. "Don't ever forget how amazing you are," he finally said. It felt lame, but he meant it. He didn't know what else to say.

She cocked her head, studying him. "You have to come get me," she said.

He frowned, confused by her comment. "Come get you from where? When?"

"When you decide you're ready for me. The ball's in your court. You have to be the one to make the next move. You know I love you. The next step is yours."

He ground his jaw, fighting against the sudden surge of hope, disbelief, and denial. The need to grab her around the waist, haul her against him, and claim her forever, was almost insurmountable. Every part of him wanted to be with her, but he fisted his hands, summoning ironclad self-control to keep himself from reaching for her. He didn't know what to say, how to express what he was feeling. "Erin—"

She held up her hand, silencing him. "There's nothing else to say. I'm going home." She took the bags from him, careful not to brush his hand with her fingers, a rejection that bit deep, so damned deep. She met his gaze. "I don't know that I could live here," she said, her gaze steady. "I don't know that I would give up my career to move out here. I don't know if I'd say yes if you came after me. But that shouldn't stop you from trying, if that's what you want to do."

He searched her face, and saw the truth in her eyes. "You really still love me?"

"Yes, I do. Just as how I'm still your everything." She smiled then, that same mesmerizing smile that he'd first seen so long ago, when she'd succeeded in talking that vet into taking the bird. She cocked her head. "I have one question, before I go."

Hope leapt through him. Hope for what, he didn't know, but definitely hope. "What's that?"

"Did you ever look for her?"

He frowned. "For who?"

"Your mom. When you got older, did you ever try to find out what happened to her? Did you ever find out why she didn't come back when she'd promised she would?"

He shrugged, his muscles tensing. "I tried. I couldn't find anything. She just took off, I guess."

She studied him. "Someone knows what happened to her. You should find out. Sometimes life isn't as hopeless as you believe it must be." She stood on her tiptoes and pressed a quick kiss to his cheek. "Good luck, Steen, with everything." She winked. "And stay out of prison, you hear?"

"Yeah, okay, for you, I'll stay clean." A brief smile flashed across his face. "Promise me, you'll beat the hell out of any man who tells you you're not good enough."

"You bet." She gave him a small salute, and then turned away. He watched her until she faded into the crowd, but she never looked back, not even once. Still, he didn't move. He waited another fifteen minutes, half-expecting to see her running back toward him through the crowds, her arms held out to him.

She didn't come, and eventually, he got back in the truck. He sat there for a few minutes, still watching the door, but she didn't appear. Grimly, he realized that she had truly walked away, without a single glance back. It was what he'd wanted, but it sucked, far more than he had ever expected. His entire soul felt heavy, as if it were being sucked into ever-deepening quicksand, and he felt exhausted, his muscles too drained to even turn the key in the ignition.

Until now, the moment he'd been declared guilty in that courtroom had been the worst moment of his life. He'd been unable to breathe, shocked that he had just been convicted of attempted murder. His entire world had started spinning, totally out of control, and only his tight grip on his chair had kept his hands from shaking violently.

But watching Erin walk away had been a thousand times worse. He felt like his soul simply withered up and died, leaving him with nothing but memories of a time when he'd once been alive. Jesus. How in the hell was he going to go on from this? What did a man do next, when the weight on his soul was too heavy to bear, and he had nowhere better to go, no hope to hang onto, and no dream to pursue?

After a long while, he numbly started the engine, and glanced back at the door one more time. A well-dressed man with silver hair walked out, and for a split-second, he thought it was Pointer's dad, who had greeted him that day when he'd gotten out of prison to thank him for saving his son's life. He realized almost immediately that he wasn't. Of course not. No one was going to walk out those doors for him today.

He started the engine and began to drive, away from the airport, away from the only woman who had ever mattered to him, except his mother.

His mother.

Erin's words about finding out what happened to her flashed through his mind, and for the first time in years, he wondered about the answers he'd never gotten. He gritted his jaw, reminding himself that it was in the past, and it didn't matter anymore.

But he could still see Erin's steady gaze as she'd told him to ask one more time. Shit. He'd wanted to prove to her that she was worthy, not to give up, but it hadn't turned out that way. She was the one who believed in him. He knew she was wrong to think he was such a great guy, but suddenly, he wanted to be the man she believed in. He wanted to make her proud, in at least one small way.

Swearing under his breath as he eased the truck to a stop at a red light, he looked down at his phone, sitting on the console beside him. After a long moment, he picked it up, and then scrolled through and found the number for Thomas Smith, Pointer's dad. He hesitated briefly, and then he pressed "Send."

A cultured woman's voice answered on the first ring. "May I assist you?"

Her voice was so refined and cultured that Steen almost

hung up. He didn't belong in that world. Then he thought of Erin, and resolution flooded him. "My name is Steen Stockton. I'm looking for Thomas Smith."

"Steen Stockton? The man who saved Pointer's life?" The woman's voice changed instantly from cool and reserved to warm and inviting.

Steen shrugged. "Yeah, well, I was there—"

"My name is Betsy Smith. That's my son whose life you saved," she said. "I will never be able to express in words how grateful I am to you. I know Pointer made a mistake that got him sent prison, but you gave him the opportunity for a second chance. He's already making plans for when he gets out. He's learned his lesson, and it's because of you, so thank you, from the bottom of my heart."

Steen leaned his head back against the seat, watching the cars cross the intersection. "You don't care that he broke the law?"

"Of course I care, but I still love him with every last bit of my heart, and I'll hug him until the end of time when he gets home again. He's my son. You never stop loving your children, no matter what. And now you're in my heart as well, forever and ever."

His throat tightening unexpectedly at the kind words, Steen drummed his fingers on the dashboard, unsettled by the discussion, and by the warmth of this woman he'd never met. He thought of his mother, who had walked out without looking back. He had to accomplish his task and then get off the phone. He wasn't used to this kind of conversation. "Is um, Thomas there, by any chance?"

"He's not, Steen, I'm so sorry. He went golfing today, and left his phone here. I thought this might be him trying to find it. I'm sure the man thinks it's lost forever. He never keeps track of this thing. Honestly, he's hopeless." Despite her words, Betsy's voice was warm with affection that made Steen think of Erin and how he felt about her. "What do you need, Steen? I might be able to help."

Suddenly, he felt stupid. What kind of person called a random stranger to ask for help? "Nothing. I was just checking to see how Pointer's doing."

"He's great, but that's not why you called," Betsy said. "I've been married for too many years, and I've raised four boys. I know what it sounds like when a man needs something and is too damned stubborn to ask for help. What do you want? I know it's not money, but we still owe you, so tell me."

The stoplight ahead of him turned green, but Steen didn't drive. Instead, he said the words he never thought he'd say. "I need some help finding someone. I don't have the resources or the contacts, but I thought maybe—"

"Thomas knows people," she said briskly. He could hear paper rustling as if she were preparing to write it down. "Who do you want to find?"

A car behind him honked, but he ignored it, his fingers tightening around the phone. "Her name is Alice Marie Rivers." He took a deep breath. "She's my mother."

❧ ❧ ❧

"Great job today, Dr. Chambers."

"Thanks, Molly." Erin wearily summoned a smile at the surgical assistant passing through the locker room as she was finishing changing after surgery. "I appreciate your help." She was tired, so tired, after the seven-hour surgery. Long surgeries were always draining, but this time, it was worse. She felt as though it had sucked every last bit of her reserves from her. It was all she could do not to simply sink down on the floor and not move ever again. It was her first surgery since her trip to Wyoming. The goal of the trip had been to rejuvenate her, giving her back the zest for life, and for *her* life in particular, but it hadn't. Despite the success of the operation, she felt the same lack of satisfaction that she'd felt before she'd left. Actually, it wasn't the *same* lack of satisfaction as before. Now, it was more like a gaping sense of meaningless misery, which was definitely not the step up she'd been hoping for.

Being away hadn't made her life better. It had made it worse, so much worse, because now she had something to compare it to: the freedom, the independence, the romance, and the realness of Wyoming. And, of course, Steen.

Now, her beautiful home on the tree-lined street felt

empty and silent without Steen there to grab her hips and molest her while she was trying to make coffee. The air felt barren and arid without the scent of horses and ranch rolling through her windows. Her patient today had been under anesthesia from the first moment to the last, so she'd never had the chance to "have a chat with it" as Steen would have done so well. It had simply been a clinical procedure, and she felt like she hadn't made any kind of meaningful difference at all, except to the wealthy owners who were hoping she could save their horse so they could continue to make money off him.

She'd been home for almost three days, and she hadn't been able to stop thinking about Steen, her phone clutched in her hand constantly, waiting for him to call and say he was on his way from the airport.

But she hadn't heard from him. Not a call, not a text, and not an email. *You are my everything.* She knew she was, which is why she hadn't really believed that he would let her walk away. When she'd told him to come after her, she'd truly thought he would.

But he hadn't.

He'd let her go, just as Louis had, and her parents. It had hurt when Louis had left. It had been devastating to grow up with parents who simply didn't care about her. But knowing that Steen was going to let her go…it hurt so deeply she felt like her heart would never again be whole.

She sighed, too tired to think. She just wanted to go home and crawl into bed. Maybe she would cancel her surgery for tomorrow. It wasn't as if she was in any shape to concentrate—

"It's my honor to assist you," Molly said cheerfully, dragging her back into the present. "Congratulations on Rising Star. It's incredible, what you did."

Erin rubbed her temples, trying not to think about how much her head was hurting. "Rising Star?" The name sounded vaguely familiar, but she was too tired to care or think. She just wanted to go home and figure out how she had gone so wrong.

Molly's eyes widened. "You didn't hear? He won the Kentucky Derby today. His career was over before you operated on him, and now he won. The procedure you did saved his career. You're going to be famous now, even more than you already are."

Erin stared at Molly, processing what she'd just said. She recalled very clearly the procedure Molly had mentioned. It had been controversial and risky, but the owner of the horse had been willing to try anything to save his investment and give the animal a chance to live up to his bloodlines. The horse had survived the surgery and recovered, but then she'd lost track of him. He'd turned out to be the winner of the Kentucky Derby, one of the most significant races around? *Wow.* "Really? When did this happen?"

"Earlier today. The owner told the press all about the surgery and how well it worked. He gave you full credit." Molly grinned. "You're going to have to open your own surgery center, Doc. There won't be space for all your cases here."

"Wow." Erin sank down onto a bench, her legs starting to tremble from exhaustion. "He told people?" She wasn't used to that. She wasn't used to anyone being proud of her. Well, anyone except Steen, who'd been proud of her simply for saving a bird. "Really?"

"Watch the news. You'll see." Molly paused with her hand on the doorknob. "You want to come out for a drink with us? To celebrate?"

Erin's heart tightened at the invitation. It was the first time she'd ever been invited by her staff. A part of her wanted to go, but at the same time, she knew she didn't belong. They were all so much younger, single, and from a different life than she was. But still, the invitation felt good. Really good. "No, thanks. Not today. Jet lag. I need to sleep. But try again next time?" Maybe next time she'd be ready to step out and try. Just not tonight. Tonight, she was still under the spell of Wyoming, Steen, and the kind of love she'd always dreamed of.

Molly's grin widened. "You bet. Have a great night." She waved as she ducked out the door, leaving Erin alone.

Wearily, Erin stood up and walked over to the sink. She rested her hands on the counter and stared at herself in the mirror, studying the bags under her eyes and the lines around the corners of her mouth. Her hair was matted from the surgical cap, hanging limply around her. God, she looked haggard and bone-weary, not like a veterinarian who had just made history. Was she really the woman who'd innovated a new procedure for racehorses who had broken bones? She didn't feel special. She just felt ordinary and empty, like something so important had slipped out of her grasp and she had no idea how to retrieve it.

She noticed little lines around the corners of her eyes. Laugh lines? She doubted it. More like self-pity crow's feet. She looked older than she remembered seeing, but as she studied herself more closely, she began to notice other changes. Her skin was flushed, not as pale as usual, with maybe a hint of tan. Her hair had light brown streaks around the temples from being outside so much visiting the farms. Her hair was less perfect, even shaggy. She looked more outdoorsy, just the tiniest bit, than she used to be. And she'd opted to put on jeans after the surgery, instead of the pleated pants she usually wore.

So, a little different...but also, in a way worse. She looked even more tired than she had before her vacation, and she felt a thousand times emptier. She felt like the blue jeans and the streaks in her hair were teasers of the brief moments of happiness she'd had with Steen and the animals, already a part of her past.

She thought of the animals she'd met in Wyoming. She'd been bitten, stepped on, and kicked. But she'd also been licked, snuggled, and gently nibbled by the furry creatures she'd worked on. Watching Steen connect with his horse that first time they'd gone riding had been so beautiful. She might know how to heal their bones, but he could heal their hearts, if only he would try. During her short vacation, she'd cried over Steen, she'd discovered passion, and she'd hugged animals who were scared of her. It had been dirty and real, completely unplanned and unpredictable...and now she was back to a life that was as sterile as her operating room.

That wasn't supposed to happen. The trip to Wyoming had been to restore her and revitalize her so she could return to her life with fresh energy and excitement. Instead, she hated being here. "Damn you, Steen," she whispered. "You showed me what my life could be like, and then you walked away."

Her phone rang. Excitement leapt through her. Had Steen seen the news and called her? She grabbed her purse and dug her phone out of it. One glance at the screen, and her heart congealed in her chest. It wasn't Steen. It was *Louis*. Her ex-husband hadn't called her since they'd finished their negotiations and finalized their divorce, except to tell her that he was coming to her family's Christmas party with his new girlfriend and he hoped she'd be okay with it.

She'd skipped the dinner.

The phone buzzed again, and she hit decline to send it to voicemail. Never again would she let him into her life.

She set the phone down and grabbed her bag to head out. As she was reaching for her purse, her cell rang again. This time, she wasn't foolish enough to have hope that it was Steen. She glanced at the screen as she was about to drop it into her purse, then stopped when she saw her dad's name on the screen.

She stared in shock at it. Her dad never called her. *Ever.* Not since the divorce, when she'd failed to hang onto her worthy husband. Her heart suddenly tightened. First Louis and then her dad? Had something happened to her mother? She grabbed the phone and answered. "Dad?"

"I think congratulations are in order." His voice boomed over the phone. "The *New York Times* has already called to talk to you. You've revolutionized equine surgery, my dear. Louis is with me, and he's been doing the interviews for you until you could get here. We're so impressed. Come to the house. We're hosting reporters here. We'll see you in ten minutes?"

"What?" She gripped the phone, trying to process. The *Times* was really interested in *her*? "Are you serious?"

"Dead serious." His voice dropped to a whisper. "Why didn't you tell me that you modified my approach to use on the horses? It was brilliant, Erin. *Brilliant.* There is huge money involved in racehorses, and you just cornered the market. Well done, my dear, *well done.* Hang on a sec. Louis wants to talk to you."

"Louis?" Her fingers tightened on the phone. Had her dad really just said "*well done*" to her? "I don't want to—"

"Erin?" Her ex-husband's slick voice made her stomach congeal. "Hey, congratulations. Great job today. I'm at your parents' house. I'd love to take you to dinner after the press conference. I want to learn more about your procedure. It's incredibly innovative and bold. I had no idea you were working on that. I'm so proud of you."

I'm so proud of you.

The words she'd been longing to hear her entire life, and now she had it. From her dad, from Louis, from everyone she'd been trying to impress for so long. She was too shocked to say anything. All she could do was hold onto the phone. It had taken public accolades and a legion of reporters, but she'd done it. She'd finally proved herself worthy.

"Erin?" Her dad came back on the line. "You coming over? I have more reporters coming. Can you be here in ten minutes? You did it, babe. *You did it.*"

She'd done it. "Okay," she finally said. "I'll be over in ten minutes."

Chapter 17

Steen's cowboy boots thudded on the wood as he walked up the front steps of Chase's ranch house. His brother had been home for half a day with his fiancée, just enough time for Steen to pack up his belongings. He was ready to go. Where, he didn't know, but he had to leave. The bunkhouse was filled with too many memories of Erin, and he couldn't stay there any longer.

He missed her so damn much that he couldn't even breathe. He'd lasted ten minutes in the bed they'd shared, and had spent the rest of the nights sleeping on a horse blanket on the floor of the bunkhouse. His back hurt like hell, which brought back memories of the fear he'd lived in when he'd first broken it, which really wasn't helping his mood.

He had to leave, and he had to leave now.

The front door of the house was open, and he could hear voices from the living room. He rapped his knuckles on the doorframe. "Chase? You around?"

"In here." His brother's voice echoed out from the living room.

Steen stepped into the ranch house with its glistening wood floors. He remembered the first time he'd been invited inside for grub, back when the ranch had been owned by Old Skip, who seemed to have made it his mission to give the Stockton boys a place to work. He was the one who'd taught Steen about horses, the one who'd shown Steen exactly how special his gift with them was. Back then, the ranch house had been falling down and worn out, but Chase had fixed it up. It looked good, good enough even for a woman like Erin.

Not that it was his house to offer her. It was Chase's.

Steen stopped in the doorway. Chase was sitting on the edge of the couch, with Mira perched next to him. They were both leaning forward, watching the television. Mira was leaning against Chase, and his hand was on her belly, as if he were staking ownership of the baby she carried. It was a scene of domesticity, one that Steen was pretty sure he'd never seen up close before.

For a moment, he imagined it was Erin sitting there, and he was parked next to her. What would that be like, to have a forever with someone? To have a kid on the way? He waited for the roil of bile in his stomach at the idea…but there wasn't any. Not even fear. He just felt…lost.

Shit. He had no room for this.

He cleared his throat and pulled his shoulders back. "You got a sec?"

Chase looked over his shoulder at him, and grinned. "Come on in. We're watching some horse racing. Mira used to watch it with her family, and she wanted to see it."

Mira looked over at him and smiled, patting the couch beside her. "Come on in, Steen."

He pulled his cowboy hat a little further down over his forehead, incredibly uncomfortable with intruding upon them and their domestic scene. "Nah, I'm good. I just wanted to tell you guys I'm leaving."

Chase's eyes narrowed, and he turned to give Steen his full attention. "Leaving where?"

"The ranch. I'm hitting the road. Gotta go somewhere."

Mira and Chase exchanged glances, then Chase stood up and strode over toward him. "Come with me. Let's talk."

Steen's jaw clenched, and he didn't move. He didn't want to get into it with his brother. "Nah, I'm good. Just wanted to say thanks for the hospitality."

Chase halted in front of him and folded his arms across his chest. "Where are you going to go?" he demanded.

"I don't know." Steen shrugged. "I'll find something."

"Working at a gas station again?" There was a challenge in Chase's voice that made Steen stiffen.

"I'll do what I have to do," he said evenly. "I'm not

going to live off your charity."

Chase swore under his breath. "Come on, Steen, you think this is charity?" He gestured toward the barn. "I need your help. I have horses in there that are so messed up that I can't help them. I've tried, and they're in just as bad a shape as when they arrived. I have two more coming in tomorrow. I spread the word that you're back, and the owners are sending their animals. These are horses that no one can help, bro. No one but you."

Steen ground his jaw, tension settling in his muscles. He'd seen horses like that before, with their wild, terrified eyes, and panicked breathing. Once he made eye contact with one of them, nothing else mattered except taking away the animal's fear and giving it the chance to reclaim its life. He shifted uncomfortably. He hadn't expected to be faced with troubled horses ever again, and he didn't have his defenses ready. "I never said I was staying."

"No, you didn't, but you want to, and I need your help. I can't run this whole damned place by myself. I'm mortgaged until I'm bleeding debt, and I have thousands of acres of unused land. I bought this place for all of us, including you."

Steen looked away, staring out the window at the vast fields. "You have seven other brothers to help you," he said quietly. "Brothers that you grew up with. You have a bond with them, not me. I came late to the party."

"Shit, Steen, really? What about the fact we all sat around your bed when you were dying in the hospital? Didn't that mean anything to you? We're all a bunch of anti-social bastards with no loyalty to anyone, except our own, and we were there for you. Not just me. Travis, Zane, Ryder, Maddox, and Quintin. Caleb wasn't there because his phone's been disconnected and we can't reach him. Logan showed up the next day, getting there as soon as he could. You got us all, Steen. When are you going to realize it?"

Steen ran his hand through his hair. A part of him wanted to believe Chase, to buy into this brotherhood crap, but he couldn't do it. He'd been down that road too many damn times, counting on people who blew him off. "I appreciate you guys were there. I do, but hell, man, I don't belong."

Chase met his gaze. "You could belong, if you got over

your shit and just let us in."

Steen stared at his half-brother, the only one of his brothers who he'd listed as an approved visitor when he'd been in prison. Suddenly, he didn't see Chase as the successful rancher. He saw the teenager who walked out onto the front porch on his third night after his mom had left. Chase had been wearing a white cowboy hat, just like now, and he'd been holding a brown one in his hand. It had been battered and worn, stinking of horse crap and sweat, and Chase had held it out to him. He'd said only one word. "Welcome." And then he'd handed Steen the hat and walked off.

Welcome.

It was the same hat that he was wearing now. Only one he'd ever worn. Only one he'd ever had. He looked at Chase, really looked at him for the first time. He'd never thought of him as a brother, not really. But he was, on some level. Maybe, just maybe—

He suddenly heard Erin's voice, and he spun around, his heart leaping. "Erin?" She wasn't behind him. He heard her talking, and he turned again, searching until he saw her face on the television. He vaulted over the back of the couch and landed beside Mira, leaning forward. Erin was wearing a tee shirt, and her hair was up in a ponytail, just as it had been so many times when she'd been out in Wyoming. She looked the same, exactly the same, and something inside him seemed to skip a beat.

She was smiling, a huge smile that lit up her whole face as she talked. "She looks good, doesn't she?" he said aloud, to no one in particular.

He was vaguely aware of Chase and Mira talking, and he waved at them to be quiet, leaning forward to hear Erin talk. He couldn't believe she was on television. He listened, riveted, as the reporter interviewed her about some surgery she'd done on the Kentucky Derby winner. Pride tightened in his chest. "Yeah," he whispered. "I knew you'd do something big." Maybe she wasn't the CEO of a major company, but this was better. This was her. This was why he didn't belong with her. What if those reporters got a hold of his past? There was no way on this earth that he'd taint her, but shit, seeing her face again, looking into her brown eyes, hearing her voice…it was too much to resist. He knew he would be lost for her forever.

This was his moment. His last hurrah with her. His everything. She was so beyond him, out of his reach, but her heart and her soul would always be a part of him.

A man moved into the camera to stand beside her. Steen narrowed his eyes when the man put his arm around Erin's shoulder, and he didn't miss her sudden tension. The man was in an expensive suit, and he looked rich as hell. The reporter asked him a question, and he started talking in some medical jargon about something, but Steen couldn't take his gaze off the man's fingers and the way they were digging possessively into Erin's shoulder.

She didn't move away from him.

And then, a banner flashed across the bottom of the screen. Doctor Louis Armstrong.

Louis.

Louis.

Her ex-husband, with his arm locked possessively around her shoulder.

Jesus.

Steen felt like his world was falling out from under him. She was back with her ex? With her *husband?* Suddenly, memories of the night with Rachel in the hotel room came flooding back. He recalled Rachel's sworn declarations that she'd never stopped loving him, his shock when a man had stumbled into the bedroom claiming to be her husband, and his numb horror when he'd watched the man fall to the ground, landing on his own knife. And he'd never forget what Rachel had said when the police arrived, pointing her finger at him and saying, *"He tried to kill my husband."*

And there Erin was, smiling into the camera, with her ex-husband's arm around her shoulder. Jesus, he knew he hadn't been good enough for her. He *knew* that, but son of a bitch, he hadn't ever thought she'd lied to him. He stumbled to his feet. "I gotta go." He had to leave. Get away. For a split second, he'd almost been convinced that he should stay, that he belonged, and it had all been a fucking mirage.

"Hey!" Chase grabbed his shoulder and Steen swung around to face him, fury boiling up inside him.

"How do you do it?" Steen snapped. "How do you sit there with Mira and pretend you know how to be family? How can you lie to her and yourself that you know anything about being a father? How can you sit on that damn couch and think you're worthy?" He snarled the words, so pissed off that Chase had the balls to pretend to be good enough. "You're just another one of old man Stockton's bastards, just like the rest of us. What makes you think you deserve that shit?"

Chase's face grew hard. "It took me a long time to think I deserved it," he said quietly, as Mira came to stand beside him, sliding her hand into Chase's callused one. "Yeah, our father was a worthless bastard who drank and beat the hell out of every one of us. Yeah, we have no idea how to be a family, but I don't care." Chase raised his and Mira's clasped hands. "All I know is that Mira believes in me, and that's enough motivation for me to do whatever I have to do to make it happen."

"You're not worthless," Mira said softly. "None of you are."

Steen looked at her, still feeling sick to his stomach. "Did you even see Erin on television? Did you see her with her husband? *Did you see her?*"

Mira looked him right in the eyes. "What I just saw was a woman who was completely uncomfortable and wanted nothing more than to get away from the man who had his arm around her. That's what I saw."

He stared at her, bracing against the sudden surge of hope in his chest. He wasn't a fool. He'd believed before. "She didn't try to get away from him."

"Did you look into her eyes?" Mira challenged.

Steen glanced back at the television screen, but the interview was over. They were showing golf now. Golf. He closed his eyes. "I can't do this again," he muttered. "I won't."

He turned away and walked out the door.

This time, his brother didn't try to stop him. Neither did Mira. They just let him go.

He didn't look back as he walked down the steps, grabbed his bag, slung it over his shoulder, and walked down the driveway.

Steen had already hiked a good mile when he heard the roar of a truck behind him, coming from the direction of the ranch house. He ground his jaw and didn't turn his head when the pickup slowed down.

"Keep the cell phone so I don't have to keep tracking you down whenever you get a phone call. Stop hiding and talk." Chase tossed the cell phone Steen had left behind at him, without even stopping.

Steen caught the phone instinctively, inhaling dirt as Chase sped up and drove away, leaving him swallowing dust.

For a long moment, he didn't even look at the phone. It had to be Erin. Who else would be calling him? He didn't know what to say. He couldn't listen to her voice and wonder how much of it had been lies, and wonder how much of a fool he'd been.

Slowly, he raised the phone to his ear. "Yeah?"

"Steen?"

It was a man's voice, one he didn't recognize. "Yeah?"

"Thomas Smith here. I took the liberty of calling this number, since this is the one you called my wife on. We didn't have any other way of contacting you. I hope that was all right."

"Thomas Smith?" The cultured voice became clearer, and he remembered Pointer's father. He stood taller. "Yes, sir, that was fine."

"You left a message with my wife. I've been working on it. Got some info for you."

Steen tightened his grip on the phone. "You mean about my mother?" A part of him wanted to hang up the phone right then. He didn't want to know. He really didn't. He'd had enough truth to last him.

"Alice Marie Rivers was a stripper and exotic dancer for ten years. A prostitute by some accounts, though details are sketchy."

Steen gritted his teeth and walked over to the nearby fence. He leaned on the wood, staring out across the dusty plains that now belonged in the Stockton family. "Yes, she was." He'd never forget the hours he'd spent sitting in one dingy motel room after another, waiting for his mother to come back with a bruise she hadn't had before. At the time, he'd been too young to understand exactly what had been going on, but he'd known it was bad, and he'd sworn every night that he'd find a way to provide for them so she didn't have to do it anymore.

He hadn't come through in time, and she'd bailed on him.

"She had one son, Steen Rivers Stockton."

He braced his palms on the fence and bowed his head, listening. "Yeah, that's her." He suddenly didn't want to hear about her life history. He knew about her life. He knew she'd had it shitty, being saddled with a kid. "Where is she now?" His fingers dug into the fence as he waited. Had she gone on to some better life? Found a rich guy who didn't want her bastard kid? Or had she met a grisly death at the hands of some john because he hadn't pulled his shit together in time to get her out of that life? "Tell me."

"She's dead, son."

Steen bowed his head against the sudden wave of grief. His eyes burned. What the hell was wrong with him? He hadn't seen her since he was a kid. That was too long to grieve the mother who'd abandoned him? "How? When?" His voice was thick and raspy, his words forcing themselves out on their own, asking questions he didn't want the answers to.

"Fourteen years ago. July fifth. Car accident. Someone was driving the wrong way on the interstate and killed her in a head-on collision. It wasn't her fault."

His gut dropped and he sucked in his breath. Killed in a car accident by a bastard driving the wrong way on the highway? What the hell? Who died like that? Then the date sank in. That had been two weeks after she'd dropped him off. "What road? Where was she going? Was it at night? Had she been drinking?"

"Late afternoon. She had just left work from her new job as an administrative assistant at a small printing company, and was, apparently, driving toward Rogue Valley."

Rogue Valley was where his father had lived, where she'd left him. She'd been driving toward *him*. Toward her kid. To get him? He closed his eyes against the emotions flooding him. Disbelief. Anger. Sadness. Relief. And...something deeper.

It was as if something deep inside him had shattered, leaving him broken and bleeding...and somehow...better. *She'd been coming back for him.* "She had a job as an admin?"

"She'd just gotten it. She'd been working there for two days."

Steen closed his eyes. His mother had been on her way back to him after finding a legit job. *She'd been coming back.* No matter how many times he thought it, it still hit like a sucker punch to the gut. All these years, he'd blamed her for leaving him, and she hadn't been. He owed her an apology, in a major way. "No one told me." His voice was raw and ragged.

"Apparently, no one knew about you. Those who knew her as a stripper didn't know she had a son, and neither did anyone at her new job. She had no other family around, so they just let her go. No one knew you existed, so there was no one to tell." Thomas sounded disgusted. "It really wasn't that hard to make the connection. I'm not impressed. I don't think anyone tried."

Steen gripped the wood, his body shaking with emotion. He had tried, and he had failed. How had he not found this out when he'd searched before? He didn't know. How different would his life have been if he'd known all those years ago that his mother hadn't ditched him? How would that have changed things? At all? Completely? He didn't even know what to think, how to process it. "Thank you, sir." He managed to keep his voice even. "I appreciate it."

"You okay, son?"

Steen lifted his head. "Yeah, fine."

"Would you like me to find out anything else about her?"

"No, that's all I need. Thanks." Steen disconnected the call, and stared across the fields. His mother had tried to come back for him. She'd left him for only two weeks. Not a lifetime. Not forever. Two weeks. She'd gotten a real job, one that he knew probably paid like shit, but she'd done it for him, for them, so they could be normal.

He let out his breath, fighting the emotion that tried to overwhelm him. For fourteen years, he thought she'd left him. She hadn't. She'd died coming back for him. He looked at his shadow on the dirt, and he saw the outline of the hat Chase had gotten him. He'd probably been wearing it the moment his mother had died.

He looked up at the sky, the endless Wyoming sky. White clouds drifted across, shifting shapes like elusive, whispered dreams. "I'm sorry, Mom," he said, his voice almost breaking. "I'm sorry I doubted you," he said, still looking at the sky. "I should have believed you when you said you loved me, instead of doubting you all these years."

There was no reply from the skies, but he felt tightness ease from his chest, as if an invisible hand had brushed across his heart and loosened the clamps that had locked his heart down for so long. He took a deep breath, a breath that seemed to spread through his entire body, gently wiping away fourteen years of torment.

She hadn't lied. She hadn't left. She hadn't betrayed him. His mom had been every bit the woman he'd thought she was.

He rested his forearms on the fence, watching as some horses came into sight in the distance while he thought about his mom, trying to call up memories of their times together. For the first time since he was a kid, the memories didn't hurt. They made him smile, as he remembered the time she'd traded an hour of braiding hair for two ice cream cones. He'd forgotten about coconut ice cream, her favorite. He'd forgotten a lot, and it felt good to let himself remember again.

A loud whinny caught his attention, and Steen focused on the horses in the distance. They were galloping, tails up, ears back, hooves pounding, the ultimate freedom to run. Those days in prison, he never thought he'd be free again. He'd been so sure he was going to die there, and when he'd taken that hit meant for Pointer, he'd been ready to die. He was glad now he hadn't. If he had, he never would have known the truth about his mom.

And he never would have gotten together with Erin. *Erin.* He wanted to call her and tell her about his mom. She would understand why it mattered. She would get it.

The horses circled toward him, the herd spreading out as they ran. Steen gradually became aware that one near the rear was slow, favoring its right foreleg. Instinctively, he let out a sharp whistle. The injured horse's head turned, and she looked right at him.

In an instant, the world seemed to stand still, until it was just him and the horse, like the old days. The mare slowed down, and then stopped, standing in the middle of the plains, still staring at him, while the rest of the herd began to slow down as well.

Steen looked over his shoulder at the long dirt road. He still had miles to go until he reached town. He'd have to keep walking if he wanted to reach it by dark. Then he looked back at the horses, who had all stopped running. They were milling about, grazing, but the injured one continued to stand still, watching him.

Shit. He thought of his mom, who hadn't walked away. He thought of what Erin had said, how he was magic with the horses. Chase had said it too. They'd both said he was needed and welcome at the Stockton ranch. Was he? They were full of shit, he was sure of it.

But then again, he'd also been damned certain that his mother had betrayed him. How much else was he wrong about?

The injured mare nickered at him.

He glared at her. "Don't start with me."

But she didn't look away, and neither did he. Shit. Did he really want to do this? Did he really want to go back to this life? As he stood there, the horse lowered its head and began to walk toward him again, still favoring her right front leg. Steen watched the mare limp toward him. She was injured and wild, and yet she was still coming to him for help.

How could he say no? He was wearing Chase's hat on his head, a welcome that he'd never accepted. Maybe it was time to accept it. Maybe it was time to pay it forward.

The mare was still twenty yards away when he dropped his bag, vaulted over the fence, and walked toward her.

They met each other halfway.

Chapter 18

The next evening Erin sat stiffly in the dining room of her parents' country club, her head ringing as she listened to her father and Louis prattle on about her great success in the Kentucky Derby. Her mother was even there, but she was more interested in discussing her own successes than worrying about what Erin had done.

So, she'd won over her dad and Louis, but not her mother.

She was dressed appropriately, in one of the silk dresses she used to wear to assorted functions she had attended with Louis. Her hair was done in a fancy updo, and she was wearing her diamond studs. She looked classy and refined, and she hated every bit of it. She didn't want to be this woman anymore. She *couldn't* be this woman anymore, not for her parents, and certainly not for Louis.

As she looked across the table at her distant mother, something inside her finally let go. The impenetrable shield that she'd held so tightly around her heart finally cracked, and she realized she didn't care anymore. "Mom."

Her mother raised her perfectly plucked eyebrows at her. "Yes, Erin?"

"I don't care if you're proud of me." God, that felt good to say.

Her mom blinked. "What?"

"I don't care." As she said it, she knew it was true. She took a deep breath, and couldn't keep the smile from turning up the corners of her mouth. "I know that you've never been impressed with my career choice." She realized Louis and her father were listening, so she expanded her circle to include them. "I know I've been a disappointment to you all—"

Her father started to interrupt. "Erin, all that has changed—"

She held up her hand. "No, it hasn't." She took a deep breath to fortify herself and looked around at them all. "I don't want to do this anymore. I don't want to be an equine surgeon. I want to be with animals who matter to people, who aren't simply about money."

The three of them stared at her blankly, completely unable to comprehend any speech that dismissed the value of money. "I'm quitting my job," she said, speaking slowly so they could understand. "I'm moving out west."

"To Wyoming?" Louis's disdain dripped from his words.

She paused as the image of Steen flashed in her mind. For a split second, she wanted to say yes. God, how she wanted to say yes. But there was no way she was going to go down that road again. She'd learned her lesson about trying to pry love from someone who didn't want to give it to her. "No, not to Wyoming. Maybe Oregon. Or Washington. Or Texas. I don't know. Somewhere. Just not here." As she said the words, she felt the most amazing sense of freedom and exhilaration. She didn't have to be this woman anymore. She didn't need their approval. A smile began to spread across her face. "I'm going to open my own clinic, in some small town where there's no other vet to take care of the animals."

Her father looked horrified. "But you've finally broken in. You're on the way to the upper echelons. Why would you ever walk away from that? Is it stress? Do you need a prescription? I can write you up a script and—"

"No, I don't need tranquilizers," she interrupted. "There's nothing wrong with me. I just don't want to do this anymore."

"Why would you do this?" Louis was staring at her with his eyes narrowed.

She could practically feel his withdrawal, and it felt brilliant. Never had disdain felt so freeing. Being rejected by people with Louis's values meant she was finally doing something right. She leaned forward so that they could all hear her. "I'm doing it, because it will make me happy."

Their blank, uncomprehending expressions in response to her announcement were all the confirmation she needed. They had absolutely no ability to grasp that simple concept. She was finished here. "I'm going home to pack." She'd given her notice yesterday, and today had been her last day. Her clinic hadn't been happy about the short notice, but that was too bad for them. It was her life, not theirs, and she was finally going to claim it.

"What about the house?" Louis caught her arm. "You're just going to leave it?"

She raised her eyebrows at him. "Do you want to buy it from me?"

"No, I want you to stay so we can work this out," he said urgently. "I made a mistake, Erin. Don't throw away your career just because you're pissed at me." He reached into his pocket and pulled out a ring, an engagement ring twice the size of her old one. "Listen, I made a huge mistake when I left you. I was a bastard, and I know it. I'm not with her anymore. I want you back. Think of what we can accomplish together."

God, how long she'd waited to hear those words, to have him beg to take her back, to see what he'd lost when he'd let her go. And now that she had it, she felt nothing. No, that was wrong. She felt disdain and disgust. "Louis—"

His gaze flicked behind her, and disdain flooded his features.

Instinctively, she turned, and her heart skipped when she saw Steen standing behind her. "Steen!" Her heart leapt at the sight, and suddenly, she couldn't breathe. He was there.

He was wearing his same battered cowboy hat, jeans that fit him just right, and cowboy boots that were still covered in dust. He looked like he'd just walked right in off the ranch, with his unshaven jaw and his plaid shirt unbuttoned at the throat. He looked rugged, dangerous, and incredibly handsome. What was he doing in Virginia? In her parents' country club? How was he even standing there?

His gaze was on Louis, not her. With a sinking heart, she realized he was staring at the engagement ring in Louis's hand.

She knew all too well how badly Rachel had betrayed him, and now, here she was, with her ex-husband handing her a diamond ring. "Steen—"

His attention leapt from the ring to her face, and she saw the hesitation in his eyes. God, is that really what he thought of her? That she'd run back to Louis after all the time she'd spent with him?

"And who is this?" Louis put his arm over her shoulders, pulling her against him in a statement of ownership. "Some ranch hand from your trip to Wyoming?"

She stiffened instinctively as anger roiled through her. She opened her mouth to snap at Louis, when Steen's expression stopped her.

He was staring at her so intently she felt as if he'd stripped her soul bare. His gaze flicked to Louis's arm, then to the huge diamond ring, and then back to her face, searching her eyes as if he could ferret out every last secret that she'd hidden inside her. Hope leapt through her, hope that maybe, just maybe, he could see her truth, that she wasn't too good for him, that she would never treat him the way everyone else in his life had treated him.

Time seemed to stand still as she waited for his reaction. She had tried so often to convince him, and finally, she realized he had to decide for himself. So, she didn't defend herself. She said nothing. She simply waited, her heart thundering as she waited for Steen to speak.

Louis stuck out his free hand, still not releasing her shoulders. "I'm Dr. Louis Armstrong, Erin's husband. Who are you?"

Steen looked at Erin. "I'm the guy who loves her."

"You are?" Tears burned in her eyes, and she couldn't keep the huge smile from lighting up her face. "You do?"

Louis's arm tightened around her. "Did you not hear me say I was her husband?"

Steen ignored Louis, instead, staring at Erin, speaking directly to her, as if Louis's arm wasn't around her and he wasn't trying to shove a massive diamond ring onto her hand. "She died," he said. "She didn't leave me. She died coming back to me. My mom."

Erin's heart softened for him. She wanted to hug him,

but she didn't move. She still didn't know why he was there, or what he wanted. "Of course she didn't leave you. What woman would ever leave you?"

"You did."

She shook her head. "You let me go. There's a difference. I tried—"

"I know." Steen suddenly reached for her, enfolding her hand in his. "I know you tried. I know you gave me your heart and your soul, but what I didn't know was that I gave mine right back to you."

She pressed her lips together, fighting against the emotions threatening to overtake her. "I knew you did. But it wasn't enough, was it?"

Steen shook his head. "That's where I was wrong." He tugged on her, pulling her away from Louis. Neither one of them acknowledged his sputter of fury as Steen took both her hands in his. "Here's the deal, Erin. My past hasn't changed. I'm still going to be living under that shadow. I can't change that. But I heard what you said about the horses. You're right. They matter to me. I'm going to work with them. It's what I need to do."

She nodded. "I'm so glad. You'll do great things for those horses." She had to ask, ask for the words she knew would never come. "Why are you here? In Virginia? At my parent's country club?"

"There are horses all over the place. Chase asked me to stay on the ranch." He shrugged, and touched the brim of his battered old hat. "I could do it, but I can't stand to be there alone. I need you with me."

Her heart seemed to come alive for the first time in her life, thundering in her chest. "You do?"

"But I won't ask you to give up your career. I saw your interview. I know you're amazing and talented, and I won't ask you to give it up. I can petition the court to move my parole to Virginia—"

"Parole?" Louis interrupted. "*Parole?* You're a convict?"

Steen's gaze flashed to Louis. "I was in prison for attempted murder," he said softly. "Don't push me."

Erin could barely stifle a giggle when she saw Louis turn ashen and hurry away to talk to her parents, who were watching the scene with shocked faces. She was sure they were horrified at the sight of Steen in his cowboy hat and jeans, and she didn't care. She looked back at Steen. "They're going to call the police. You should go."

"I got permission to leave the state. Pointer's dad pulled some strings for me. It turns out, saving his son's life made him like me, and the man has connections." He cradled her hands against his chest, searching her face. "Here's the thing, Erin. I know you're a thousand times more than what I could ever be, and I can't offer you country club dinners, but I can swear on my mother's soul to love you the way you deserve to be loved. I will always stand by you, I will always be proud of you, and I will always be the best man I can be for you. I will always, without fail, love you with every last bit of my heart. I've loved you since you were fourteen years old, and I will love you until the end of time."

This time, she couldn't stop the tears from falling. "I love you, too, Steen."

He went down on one knee, and took her hand in his. "I will be yours in whatever way you'll have me. If you want me to walk away, I will. If you want me to move to Virginia, I'm on it. If you want to live on the ranch with me, I'll build you the best damned house anyone ever lived in."

She knew what her answer was, oh, she knew, but before she answered, she had to ask him. "When did you realize that what you can give me is enough?"

He looked up at her. "When I realized that my mom had died for me. She didn't need to get a real job for me. Just her alone would have been enough. All I wanted was for her to love me. Her love would have been enough for me, which made me realize that maybe, just maybe, my love would be enough for you."

She went down on her knees so she was level with him and framed his handsome face with her hands. "Being loved by the person you love isn't simply enough. It's everything."

For the first time, hope hovered in his eyes, chasing away the shadows that had been haunting them for so long. "You're my everything, Erin. I love you."

"You're my everything, Steen. You always have been."

Her throat was tight, but she knew she had to get out the words before she was crying too much to talk. "I just told my parents I was quitting my job and moving west to open a regular vet clinic. I need a place to live, and a roommate to split the bills." She wrapped her arms around his neck. "I pick you."

Disbelief swept over his face. "Really? You want to move to the ranch with me?"

She grinned. "Really. If you'll have me."

"Damn woman. I'd have given my soul for another minute with you. To have you with me forever? It's more than I could ever have dreamed. Before you, I didn't even know this existed." He pressed his palm over her heart. "Love, passion, commitment, trust. You showed it to me, and you taught me to believe." He slipped his hands into her hair, gently tugging her closer to him. "I've been waiting for you my whole life, bird girl." Then he kissed her, a kiss that was so private, and so personal, and so beautiful that she knew she had finally found where she belonged: in the arms of the man who had won her heart so many years ago.

Chapter 19

Steen paused in the doorway of Chase's living room, taking a moment to survey the scene. Mira and Erin were sitting side by side on the couch, going over paint swatches. Mira's belly was enormous now, and Steen half-expected that baby to pop out at any second, though his brother assured him they still had another couple months to go. Chase was leaning back in the easy chair, with a glass of lemonade in his hand, watching the women with the most satisfied expression on his face.

Steen knew that expression, because he felt the same way. So damned happy. He never thought he'd walk into Chase's living room and feel comfortable, but he did. He loved coming in here and knowing that he belonged, that he was slowly building connections he'd never had before.

It would take time, but it felt good. Really damn good. And it was all because of Erin.

It was a familial scene, one with women's laughter and pastel colors for the baby's nursery. There was a fire in the fireplace, and pictures on the mantle. It was a place he never, ever thought he'd be, but with Erin to support him, he was learning how to navigate it.

Granted, his favorite time of the day was retiring to the bunkhouse each evening with Erin, but a few dinners with his brother and Mira weren't so bad. Not bad at all, in fact.

As he stood there with drinks in his hand, Erin looked up. She immediately smiled, the kind of warm, just-for-him smile that always melted his heart. He grinned back and walked into the room. He handed Mira her lemonade, then sat next to Erin and gave her the glass of wine he'd poured for her.

Yeah, there wasn't much space on the couch, but he needed to be beside her. He always needed to be beside her, touching her, talking to her. He wanted her input in the plans for their new house, and for the vet clinic he was going to attach to it. Of course, Josie already had her clinic in town, but she'd been thrilled to have Erin set up shop. Apparently, she hadn't been able to keep up with the demand, and there was plenty of market share.

Erin held up a pale pink color swatch. "What do you think of this?"

He raised his brows. "I thought it was a boy. Not sure he'll be okay with that."

She rolled her eyes. "Not for them. For us."

He stared at her, and his gut suddenly dropped out of his stomach. "For *us*? Are you—" His gaze dropped in shock to her belly, and a thousand emotions rushed through him.

Her face paled. "No. I meant for the waiting room at the clinic."

"Oh." He couldn't stop the crash of disappointment that plummeted through him.

She stared at him. "I thought you wanted to wait until you were done with your parole and were totally free before we got married or had children. Did you want me to be pregnant just then?"

"Shit, yeah. I mean, yeah, to wait. But—" He jerked his gaze to hers. "When you just said...I thought..." He spread his hands. "I don't know. It just...the thought of you being a mom... it felt right."

Her face softened. "And what about you being a dad? How did that feel?"

Steen looked across the room at his brother, feeling helpless. What the hell did he know about being a parent? Chase nodded once, grinning at him "You'll figure it out." As Chase spoke, Mira got up, walked over to him, and snuggled into his lap.

His brother rested his hand possessively on Mira's belly and pressed a kiss to her hair. "It's all good, bro. You'll be fine."

Steen looked back at Erin, who was watching Mira and Chase with a wistful expression on her face. He'd never seen such stark longing, and a part of his gut twisted up. "Erin." He spoke softly, just for her.

She turned back toward him, and the wistfulness was gone, replaced with the same look of tenderness she always reserved just for him. "Yes?"

"I'm so sorry we're not married yet."

The wistfulness came back into her eyes. "Steen. I would marry you in a heartbeat, but I understand that your sense of honor guides you. You want to give me a chance to leave if your past becomes too much." She tucked her feet up beneath her as she slipped her hands around his neck. "You need to understand that you could be on parole for the rest of your life, and I will never leave you." She took his hand and placed it over her heart. "You're my home, Steen. You're my heart. You're my everything. I spent my life waiting for people to look at me with the respect I wanted, and I almost destroyed myself in my effort to impress others. I don't care about that anymore. I just care about the man I love."

Steen's throat tightened, and his eyes suddenly felt like they were burning. "How did I get so lucky to find you?"

She shrugged. "It took kind of a long time. It wasn't exactly easy."

"No, it wasn't." He slipped his finger beneath her chin and kissed her lightly. "It was worth everything I endured, because it made me end up with you." He pushed her hair behind her ears, staring down into the face of the only person in the world who mattered to him, though Chase and Mira were starting to claim their space. None of the other Stocktons had come by yet, and he wasn't sure how he'd feel when they showed up, but he was willing to try. But in the meantime.... "I swear I'll marry you," he said, pressing a kiss to Erin's lips. "I bought the ring." His heart lifted when he saw her face light up. "I'm just waiting until I can give it to you, but I needed to have it." He needed the tangible reality of their future that the ring gave him, but he couldn't give it to her yet. He needed her to be free to leave him, and he couldn't give her the ring until he knew that she would never want to walk away from the baggage he brought with him.

"Don't tell her you bought a ring," Mira protested. "That takes all the surprise out of it. A woman needs romance."

"Like being proposed to in a tree?" Chase teased. "Was that romantic enough for you?"

She giggled at him, and whispered something to Chase that had them both laughing and whispering.

Steen kept his focus on Erin. "When Chase and Mira get married in a few weeks, it might make you uncomfortable, but I don't want you to doubt how I feel about you. I want you to be certain of my intentions." He still couldn't believe all his brothers except Caleb would be coming for the wedding. He wasn't ready to face them yet.

She nodded. "I do know, but I appreciate you telling me. It feels good to hear it aloud." Her eyes sparkled. "Can I peek at the ring?"

He grinned. "No, of course not—"

A heavy knock sounded on the front door, and Steen tensed. "Zane?" he guessed. Zane was the brother most likely to stop by, but he hadn't heard the roar of his motorcycle.

"I don't know. It's late." Chase started to untangle himself from Mira, but Steen stood up. "I'll get it."

He had to face his brothers at some point. He had to learn who they were. He strode across the door and pulled it open.

It wasn't Zane.

It was Thomas Smith, Pointer's dad. He was wearing pressed jeans and a sweater, but his dress shirt was untucked, as if he'd barely managed to pull himself together before heading out. Steen's first thought was of the young man they both knew. "Is Pointer okay? You need something?"

He ignored Steen's questions. "May I come in?" The cultured tones of Thomas's voice no longer felt so threatening to Steen. He knew that Thomas was on his side, and the man was willing to throw considerable weight around for him.

"Of course." He stepped back as Erin and the others stood up. "This is my brother, Chase Stockton, his fiancée Mira Cabot and my..." He met Erin's gaze. "My..." He wanted to say fiancée. Wife. Anything to show how special she was. Girlfriend seemed pathetically inadequate, and he wouldn't say fiancée until she was wearing his ring. So, he simply settled for her name. "Erin Chambers." His fiancée. He wanted to say it, but he didn't dare. It wasn't fair to her. All he could offer was the tone of his voice when he said the words, as if he could somehow inject into her name how deeply he felt about her. He knew it wasn't enough, but he couldn't take more from her, not yet. He instinctively glanced at Erin's face to make sure she was okay with it.

Her smile said she was, as did the way she slipped around the end of the couch and walked over to stand beside him, gently sliding her hand into his. Steen grinned at the man.

Thomas smiled at Erin. "So this is the woman you ran off to Virginia to track down. I guess it paid off."

Steen grinned. "Yeah, it did. She took me back."

"Glad to hear it."

"Thank you, sir. I really appreciate it."

Thomas rolled his eyes. "Don't call me 'sir.' Just Thomas."

Steen nodded. Thomas was a man who had always been so far above him in life, and now he was just Thomas. It felt good, really good. "Can I offer you a drink?"

"Hell, no. I need to get going." Thomas's blue gaze settled on Steen's. "I've been working all my contacts to try to get Pointer's conviction overturned. He's a good kid, and he got caught up in the aftermath of my work. He made a mistake, but it wasn't his fault, and I was willing to do whatever it took to get him out of there."

Hope leapt through Steen. "Is that why you're here? Is Pointer free?"

"He sure is." A broad grin broke over Thomas's face. "I'm on my way now to pick him up."

Steen grinned. "That's fantastic."

"Yes, it is." Thomas's smile faded. "But if you hadn't saved his life, it would have been too late. I owe you."

Steen put his arm around Erin and pulled her against him. "No, you don't. We're even. I got the girl. We both got the one we loved. We're more than even."

"Not yet." Thomas held out a folded paper. "When I had my team researching your mother, we uncovered a lot more about you. The truth."

Steen frowned as he took the paper. "What are you talking about?"

"You didn't try to murder anyone. You know it, the lying bastard knows it, and now the governor knows it."

"What?" Steen stared at the older man. "What are you talking about?"

Thomas just nodded at the paper. "Open it."

Steen slowly, disbelievingly, unfolded the paper. Erin leaned over his arm, reading with him. He saw the letterhead. He saw his name. He saw the word *pardoned.* And the word *innocent.* Erin made a small noise of disbelief, and Steen felt his whole body begin to shake. He stared at Thomas. "What is this?"

"You're a free man, Steen. You've been pardoned. It's over." He met his gaze. "I could have asked for a retrial, but those take time and anything can happen. I wanted it over. The governor pardoned you based on several private, off-the-record, confessions to the governor at his home that I…facilitated." He winked, leaving no doubt that those private confessions had not been obtained easily. "The other parties involved are now being investigated for perjury, but I wouldn't hold my breath. Her father has considerable influence." Thomas grinned. "Not as much as I have, though."

Steen felt like his head was spinning, and his hand was shaking. He'd been pardoned. His record expunged. No parole. No conviction. Nothing. Just a new life of complete freedom. "I don't know what to say—"

"There's nothing to say," Thomas said. "It still doesn't repay my debt to you." He nodded at the others. "I have to go get my kid," he said. He held out his hand. "It would be my honor to consider you a friend, Steen."

Steen didn't hesitate. He shook Thomas's hand. "The honor is mine, sir... Thomas."

Thomas said his farewells to the rest of the crew, and then jogged down the stairs to a black Mercedes idling in the driveway.

Steen didn't even bother to close the front door. He simply turned to Erin, took her hand, and went down on one knee. "Will you marry me?" He wanted to say a million things, to tell her how much he loved her, to shout to the world the gift that Thomas had just given him, but in that moment, he wanted only one thing, for Erin to be his wife, so he could hold onto her forever.

Her eyes shimmered with unshed tears. "Of course I will. You didn't need to be pardoned for me to marry you."

"I know I didn't, but I needed to be the man you deserve." He dug into his front pocket and held up the diamond ring he'd bought on his way to Virginia. He'd had it in his pocket since that day, always prepared to show it to her if she began to doubt his intentions. Never in a million years had he thought he'd have the chance to give it to her so soon. "I know it's not as big as the one Louis gave you—"

"It's perfect." Her whisper was so full of emotion and love, that he knew it was. She held out her hand, and he slipped the ring onto her finger. The diamond glittered like the stars on a summer night, and he pressed a kiss to the sparkling stone.

She held out her arms to him, and he rose to his feet, pulling her into the fold of his body. He kissed her, their first kiss as an engaged couple, and it was a thousand times more perfect than all the other perfect ones they'd shared. Her body felt amazing, incredible, and perfect against his. He broke the kiss, whispering in her ear. "Let me take you back home. I need to make love to my fiancée," he whispered.

She beamed up at him, her face glowing with happiness. "Yes, please do."

He looked over her shoulder at Chase and Mira, who were beaming at them. "I think we're going to head out. Thanks for dinner."

"Not yet." Chase held up his hand, exchanging glances with Mira, who nodded. Then both of them looked at Steen and Erin. "We'd be honored if you guys wanted to do a double wedding with us. I know it's soon, but not really. It's been a long time for you guys. No pressure, but the invite's open."

Rightness roared through Steen, and he knew that he wanted nothing more than to marry Erin as soon as possible. He looked down at her, and his heart softened when he saw the expression on her face.

He took her hand and pressed a kiss to her palm. "I've

been waiting for you for years," he said softly. He'd been willing to wait for as long as it took to make himself worthy of her, but now that Thomas has purged his past, now that he had the opportunity, his entire soul was burning for her, to make her his, forever. "I'd marry you tonight, if I could. I know that you probably want your own wedding, and that's cool. I'll wait as long as it takes, but—"

"Yes."

He broke into a grin. "Yes? Yes, to the double wedding?"

She grinned. "Of course, yes. I think we've waited enough years, don't you?"

"Hell, yeah." He let out a whoop and swung her in his arms, unable to wipe the grin off his face. He grinned stupidly at his brother and Mira. "You guys sure? I mean—"

"Family, man." Chase walked over. "It's all about family." Then his big brother dragged Steen into a bear hug. For a split second, Steen hesitated, then he felt Mira's arms go around him and Chase, locking them together. Steen wrapped one arm around his soon-to-be sister-in-law, and then held out his other arm to Erin.

She came willingly, sliding into his embrace and into the circle of the family that he was no longer willing to run away from. He couldn't turn them away. It just felt too damn good to be a part of it, and he knew that it was Erin who had given him the strength to reach out and be willing to try.

"I love you," he whispered to her.

She smiled up at him. "I love you, too, cowboy. Always and forever."

The best damn words he'd ever heard.

Sneak Peek: A Real Cowboy Rides a Motorcycle

A *Wyoming Rebels* Novel

He was tired.

He was cranky.

He was wet.

Zane Stockton idled his motorcycle outside his brother's ranch house, narrowing his eyes at the darkened windows. Gone was the time when he'd let himself in and crash. There was a woman in there now, and that changed all the rules, especially when it was two in the morning.

He probably shouldn't have come tonight, but he was here, and he was done being on the road for now. Rain had been thundering down on him for hours, and he was drenched all the way to his bones. He just wanted to sleep and forget about all the crap that had gone down today.

Trying not to rev the engine too much, he eased his bike down the driveway past the barn and turned right into the lean-to beside the bunkhouse. He settled his bike and whipped out a couple towels to clean it off, making sure it was mud-free before calling it a night.

He grabbed his bag from the back of the bike, scowling when he realized it had gotten wet, then sloshed across the puddles toward the front door of the bunkhouse. He retrieved the key from the doorframe, and pried the thing open.

It was pitch dark inside, but he knew his way around and didn't bother with a light. He dropped the bag, kicked off his boots and his drenched clothes, then headed for the only bed that was still set up in the place, ever since Steen and Erin had rearranged it for their own use during their temporary stay there. At least they'd upgraded their lodging so the bunkhouse was now available again for use by the family vagrant.

Zane jerked back the covers and collapsed onto the bed. The minute he landed, he felt the soft, very real feel of a body beneath him, including the swell of a woman's breast beneath his forearm. Shit! "What the hell?" He leapt to his feet just as a woman shrieked and slammed a pillow into the side of his head.

"Hey, I'm not going to hurt you! I'm Chase's brother!" He grabbed the pillow as it clocked him in the side of the head again. "Stop!"

There was a moment of silence, and all he could hear was heavy breathing. Then she spoke. "You're Chase's brother?" Her voice was breathless, and throaty, as if he'd awakened her out of a deep sleep, which he probably had. It sounded sexy as hell, and he was shocked to feel a rush of desire catapult through him.

Shit. He hadn't responded physically to a woman in a long time, and now he'd run into a woman who could turn him on simply by *speaking* to him? Who the hell was she? "Yeah," he said, sounding crankier than he intended. "Who are you?"

"You're Steen?" He heard her fumbling for something, and he wondered if she was searching for a baseball bat, pepper spray, or something that indicated she hadn't been nearly as turned on by his voice as he'd been by hers.

"No, a different brother," he replied, his head spinning as he tried to figure what was going on, and why he was reacting to her so intensely. "I'm Zane. Harmless. Good guy. No need to decapitate me."

There was a pause in her movements. "I wasn't going to decapitate you. I was looking for my shirt."

"Your shirt?" he echoed blankly. "You're not wearing a shirt?" He hadn't noticed much bare skin for that brief moment he'd been on top of her. How had he missed it?

"I'm wearing a camisole, but it's not exactly decent. Give me a sec." A small laugh drifted through the darkness. "You're such a guy. Of course you'd fixate on the possibility of me being naked. Do all men think only of sex?"

He grinned, relaxing. He'd startled her, but she'd regrouped quickly, and he liked that. She wasn't a wimp who was running to the door screaming. "What's your name?" he asked.

"Taylor Shaw. I'm Mira's best friend from home. I surprised her for a visit, but it turns out, there's no space in the house."

"Nope. Not anymore. I'm displaced too." He suddenly wanted to see her. "You decent yet?"

"Yes, but barely—"

He reached over and flicked on the small light by the bed. The soft yellow glow was less harsh than the overhead light, but it still took his eyes a moment to adjust to the brightness. When they did, he saw Taylor sitting on the bed, curly blond hair tumbling around her shoulders in a disheveled mess that made her look completely adorable. Her eyes were green, fixed on him as she squinted against the sudden light. He could see the curve of her shoulders beneath the light pink, long-sleeved shirt she was wearing. The faint outline of a white camisole was evident beneath her shirt, not quite obscuring the fact that she wasn't wearing a bra. Her gray yoga pants were frayed at the knee and cuff, but they fit her hips with perfection. She looked like she'd just tumbled right out of a bed, and she was sexy as hell.

But it was her face that caught his attention. Her gaze was wary, but there was a vulnerability in it that made him want to protect her. He had zero protective instincts when it came to women...until now, until he'd met this woman who'd tried to defend herself with a pillow.

Then her gaze slid down his body, and his entire body went into heated overdrive. It wasn't until her eyes widened in horror when her gaze was at hip level that he remembered something very important.

He was naked.

Sneak Peek: Shadows of Darkness

An *Order of the Blade* Novel

Levi Hart froze, his senses shocked into hyper-awareness when he caught the unmistakable scent of a *woman.* It plunged past his shields, invading his being with a force so strong he had no chance to protect himself from the sheer intensity of her presence. He swore and went utterly still. His mind went into hyper-focus as he fought to regain control, his body barely swaying on the ancient meat hook he'd been chained to for over a century.

But with each breath he took, the fragile, delicate scent of pure femininity wrapped itself tighter around him. Hot. Sensual. Tempting. And utterly dangerous to a Calydon warrior who was driven by a dark, powerful need for a woman.

His ancient instincts rose fast and hard, a driving lust that he hadn't succumbed to in centuries. Swearing under his breath, he closed his eyes, summoning what was left of his once formidable discipline to regain control of his body and his senses. It took precious seconds to shut down the lust burning through him. He had to engage strength he couldn't afford to waste in order to crush the almost insurmountable need to find her *right then,* but he did it.

The relief was instant, but a residue of emptiness resonated through him, as if his very being was stumbling in the absence of that sexual hunger. Without the distraction, however, a sharp-edged focus settled over him. He narrowed his eyes and called upon his preternatural senses, sending waves of psychic energy out into the surrounding tunnels, searching for the physical presence of the woman he had scented.

He found nothing.

A dark fury raged through him, anger that he couldn't find her. Urgency mounted, and he sent out another wave of energy, but this time, he opened his mind, sending the tentacles of his consciousness out into the air, searching with ruthless speed. Within seconds, he picked up her feminine energy again. This time, he kept his physical response contained, and he allowed his mind to hurtle toward her at a mind-numbing pace, racing through tunnels and around corners, faster and faster, gaining speed with each millisecond, her scent becoming stronger and stronger until—

He found her.

The moment his mind touched hers, she sucked in her breath, and her mind snapped to his, injecting warmth and passion into his cold, isolated being. His entire body clenched in response, and tension radiated through his muscles as he fought to concentrate. She smelled of spring and outdoors, of grass, of nature, and of a lazy sensuality, things he hadn't experienced in over a hundred years. But since he'd opened his mind to her, it wasn't simply her physical being he accessed. Her emotions assaulted him, a dizzying onslaught of fear, courage, and desperation, all of it ruthlessly contained by her single-minded focus and determination. His name reverberated through her mind, and it was layered through her entire being.

All her attention was centered on *him.*

His body responded to the knowledge, a tightening of his cock that he couldn't control no matter how hard he fought it. To have his name and his existence so intricately woven into the fabric of her being was so visceral that he could almost feel her presence, as if she was right in front of him. He couldn't keep his physical response contained, and his lust spilled over their connection into her. Instantly, desire flooded her, and he felt her body respond to his.

The connection between them was electric and intense, igniting his cells like fire licking its way through his body. He was a cold-blooded assassin who'd spent a lifetime honing his utter lack of emotion and eradicating his need for physical connection with a woman, and yet, in mere seconds, she'd stripped away every last defense and created a need in him so powerful he knew he'd be sprinting through the tunnels in search of her if he weren't locked down.

Who the hell was she? And why was she there? No one had set foot in any of the caverns surrounding his prison since he'd been chained up, and he didn't believe it was a coincidence that she was so close, thousands of feet below the surface of the earth in tunnels that no human being would ever stumble across, thinking about him. *Who are you?* He pressed the question at her, instinctively erecting a telepathic bridge between their minds.

She froze in response, and for a split second, he felt her confusion that he was speaking in her mind. Then fear rippled through her, and she slammed up her mental shields, severing their link. Emptiness assaulted him at the lack of connection, and he swore, struggling to regain his equilibrium. She'd cut him off, but he knew she'd heard him.

She'd heard him. After more than a century of complete isolation, *she'd heard him.* The sudden shock of having his existence recognized by another living creature hit him with an almost violent crash of emotion. His entire being suddenly burned with a need to be acknowledged, to be recognized, to be *seen.*

He shoved aside the emotions before they had a chance to claim him. He'd lived his whole life alone. He'd been a shadow in the night, a phantom who was everyone's worst nightmare. His solitary existence had never bothered him, not even for an instant, and he wasn't going to let it start grating on him now just because he'd been strung up like a carcass for a century and had scented a woman so enticing it could drive him mad if he let it consume him.

Her essence became stronger, and he realized she was headed right for him, on a direct path through the tunnels. *She was seeking him out.* Anticipation burned through him, an escalating need to see her, to hear her voice, to drag her against him and taste her mouth against his.

He swore and closed his eyes, raising his own shields to block her scent so he could recalibrate. What the hell? Why was he reacting like that to her? Was it just because he'd been isolated for so long? Or maybe she was some sort of seductress? Not that it mattered. He didn't want to make out with her. He wanted to *escape.*

This might be his chance.

He took a deep breath, summoning the combat-focus that had once been as instinctual as breathing and staying alive. Decades of no food, no water, and no external stimulation had weakened him, and his mind fought against his commands to concentrate so intently.

With a snarl of fury, he forced his mind to respond, channeling what was left of his strength into his mind until it coalesced into the razor-sharp clarity that had once defined him.

Straining to see in the darkness, he scanned the cave that had been his prison for so long. It had taken years for his eyes to adjust to the rampant darkness enough for him to be able to see anything, and even now, he could make out only the faintest dark shapes that indicated tunnel openings, escape routes that were only yards away, and yet completely out of reach.

She was in one of those tunnels, getting closer with each step.

Manipulating his body weight with the effortless grace of a man who'd spent countless hours figuring out how to stay fit and strong even while he was suspended by his wrists in a frigid, underground cave, Levi spun in a circle. He systematically inspected every inch of his cave, searching for indications that would tell him which direction she was approaching from.

Unable to resist the temptation, he inhaled again, and her scent wrapped around him, diffusing through his cells like a tendril of sunshine in a body that had long been dead. Energy pulsed through him, a sense of vitality he hadn't felt in decades. He reached out to her again, this time searching the space around her for more information on who she was. With his attention no longer only on her, he noticed the presence of two powerful males flanking her.

His hands clenched, and his muscles went taut. *She was with two Calydon warriors.* Possessiveness surged through him, a sudden fear for her safety. Was she their prisoner? Were they going to lock her up the way he'd been strung up? Suddenly, it was no longer about sex. It was no longer about his need to be acknowledged. It became only about protecting her. *Are you in danger?* He pressed the question ruthlessly at her mind, shattering her mental shields.

Again, she flinched, clearly hearing him, but once again, she didn't answer. Instead, she thrust him out of her mind as efficiently as he'd penetrated it.

He had to admit, he was impressed with her defenses, but at the same time, it was annoying as hell. He had no idea what the situation was. Did he need to protect her? Was she in danger?

No. No. *No.*

His job wasn't to protect *anyone.* He had one last mission to accomplish, and he couldn't afford to get distracted by a woman. He had to escape, hunt down the man who had nearly destroyed Levi's soul…and then kill him. He could allow the approaching threesome to mean only one thing to him: a chance to gain his freedom.

Sneak Peek: Prince Charming Can Wait

An *Ever After* Novel

Clouds were thick in the sky, blocking the moon. The lake and the woods were dark, swallowing up light and life, like a soothing blanket of nothingness coating the night. Emma needed to get away from the world she didn't belong to, the one that held no place for her. Tears were thick in her throat, her eyes stinging as she ran. The stones were wet from the rain earlier in the day, and the cool dampness sent chills through her.

She reached the dock and leapt out onto the damp wood. Her foot slipped, and she yelped as she lost her balance—

Strong hands shot out and grabbed her around the waist, catching her before she fell into the water. Shrieking in surprise, she jerked free, twisting out of range. The evasive move sent her off balance again, her feet went out from under her, and she was falling—

And again, someone grabbed her. "Hey," a low voice said. "I'm not going to hurt you."

Emma froze at the sound of the voice she knew so well, the one that had haunted her for so many sleepless nights. The voice she thought she'd never hear again, because he'd been gone for so long. "Harlan?"

"Yeah."

Emma spun around in his grasp, and her breath caught as she saw his shadowed face. His eyes were dark and hooded in the filtered light, his cheek bones more prominent than they had been the last time she'd seen him. Heavy stubble framed his face, and his hair was long and ragged around the base of his neck. He was leaner than she remembered, but his muscles were more defined, straining at his tee shirt. He looked grungy and real, a man who lived by the earth every day of his life. He exuded pure strength and raw appeal that ignited something deep within her. She instinctively leaned toward him, into the strength that emanated from him. His hands felt hot and dangerous where they clasped her hips, but she had no urge to push him away.

Damn him. After not seeing him for nearly a year, he

still affected her beyond reason.

"You're back," she managed.

"Yeah."

Again, the one word answer. He had never said much more than that to her, but she'd seen him watching her intently on countless occasions, his piercing blue eyes roiling with so much unspoken emotion and turbulence. She managed a small smile, trying to hide the intensity of her reaction to seeing him. "Astrid didn't mention you would be here."

"She doesn't know." Again, he fell silent, but he raised one hand and lifted a lock of her hair, thumbing it gently. "Like silk," he said softly. "Just as I always thought it would feel."

Her heart began to pound now. There was no way to stop it, not when she was so close to him, not when she could feel his hands on her, a touch she'd craved since the first time she'd seen him. It had been two years ago, the day she'd walked back into her life in Birch Crossing. He had been leaning against the deli counter in Wright's, his arms folded over his chest, his piercing blue eyes watching her so intently.

And now he was here, in these woods, holding onto her.

His grip was strong, but his touch was gentle in her hair as he filtered the strands through his fingers. "You've thought about my hair before?" she asked. Ridiculous question, but it tumbled out anyway. And she wanted to know. Had he really thought about her before? Was she not alone in the way her mind had wandered to him so many nights when she hadn't been able to sleep?

His gaze met hers, and for a second, heat seemed to explode between them. Then he dropped his hands and stepped back. The loss of his touch was like ice cold water drenching her, and she had to hug herself to keep from reaching out for him.

"Tell Astrid I was here," he said. "I'm leaving again—"

"What?" She couldn't hold back the protest. "Already? Why?"

"I have a job."

That job. That mysterious job. He had never told Astrid, or anyone else in town, where he went when he disappeared. Sometimes, he was in town for months, playing at his real estate business, taking off for only a few days at a time. Other times, he was absent for longer. This last time, he'd been gone for almost a year, which was the longest that anyone could remember him being away. And he was leaving again already? "Astrid misses you," Emma said quickly, instinctively trying to give him a reason not to disappear again. "You can't leave without at least saying hi."

Harlan's gaze flickered to the house, and his mouth tightened. He made no move to join the celebration, and suddenly she realized that he felt the same way she did about invading that happy little world. He didn't belong to it any more than she did. Empathy tightened her chest, and she looked more carefully at the independent man who no one in town had ever been able to get close to. "You can stop by and see her tomorrow," she said softly.

He didn't move, and he didn't take his eyes off the house. "She's happy? Jason's good to her?"

Emma nodded. "He treasures her. They're so in love." She couldn't quite keep the ache out of her voice, and she saw Harlan look sharply at her.

"What's wrong?" he asked. "Why did you say it like that?"

"No, no, they're great. Really." She swallowed and pulled back her shoulders, refusing to let herself yearn for that which she did not want or need in her life. "She would kill me if she found out I let you leave town without seeing her. How long until you have to go?"

He shifted. "Forty-eight hours." The confession was reluctant.

"So, then, come back here tomorrow and see her," she said, relief rushing through her at the idea that he wasn't leaving town immediately. For at least two nights, she could sleep knowing that he was breathing the same air as she was.

"No, not here." He ran his hand through his hair, and she saw a dark bruise on the underside of his triceps. "You guys still go to Wright's in the morning for coffee?"

Emma's heart fluttered at his question. For a man who had held himself aloof, he seemed endearingly aware of what his sister did every day...and he knew that she was always there as well. "Yes. We'll be there at eight thirty."

He nodded. "Yeah, okay, I'll try to make it then." He glanced at her again, and just like before, heat seemed to rush through her—

Then he turned away, stealing that warmth from her before she'd had time to finish savoring it. "No." She grabbed his arm, her fingers sliding over his hard muscles. Shocked by the feel of his body beneath her palm, she jerked back, but not soon enough.

He froze under her touch, sucking in his breath. Slowly, he turned his head to look back at her. "No?"

"Don't *try* to make it tomorrow morning," she said quickly, trying to pretend her panic had been on Astrid's behalf, not her own. "You *have* to make it. Astrid needs to see you. She wants you to meet Rosie. She's happy, Harlan, but she needs her brother, too. Jason is her family, but so are you, and you know how she needs to be connected."

Harlan closed his eyes for a long moment, and she saw emotions warring within him. For a man so stoic and aloof, he was fermenting with emotions in a way that she'd never seen before. She looked again at the bruise on his arm. "Are you okay, Harlan? What happened while you were gone?" There was no way to keep the concern out of her voice, no way to hide that her heart ached at the thought of him being hurt.

His eyes opened again. He said nothing, but he suddenly wrapped his hand around the back of her neck.

She stiffened, her heart pounding as he drew her close to him. "What are you doing?"

"I need this." Then he captured her mouth with his.

She had no time to be afraid, no time to fear. His kiss was too desperate for her to be afraid. It wasn't a kiss to seduce or dominate. It was a burning, aching need for connection, for humanity, for something to chase away the darkness hunting him...everything she needed in a kiss as well.

Her hands went instinctively to his chest, bracing, protecting, but at the same time, connecting. She kissed him back, needing the same touch that he did, desperate for that feeling of being wanted. She didn't know this man, and yet, on some level, she'd known him for so long. She'd seen his torment, she'd felt his isolation, and she'd witnessed his unfailing need to protect Astrid, even if he had never inserted himself fully into her life.

Somehow, Harlan's kiss wasn't a threat the way other men's were. He was leaving town, so he was no more than a shadow that would ease into her life and then disappear. He wouldn't try to take her, to trick her, to consume her. He wouldn't make promises and then betray them. All he wanted was the same thing she did, a break from the isolation that locked him down, a fragile whisper of human connection to fill the gaping hole in his heart.

"Emma!" Astrid's voice rang out in the night, shattering the moment. "Are you out here?"

Harlan broke the kiss, but he didn't move away, keeping his lips against hers. One of his hands was tangled lightly in her hair, the other was locked around her waist. Somehow, he'd pulled them close, until her breasts were against his chest, their bodies melted together. It felt so right, but at the same time, a familiar anxiety began to build inside Emma at the intimacy.

"Do not fear me, sweet Emma," Harlan whispered against her lips. "I would only treasure what you give."

His voice was so soft and tender that her throat tightened. How she'd yearned for so many years, for a lifetime, for someone to speak to her like that…until she'd finally become smart enough to relinquish that dream. And now, here it was, in the form of a man who would disappear from her life in forty-eight hours, maybe never to return. Which was why it was okay, because she didn't have to worry that he would want more than she could give, or that she would give him more than she could afford. Maybe she didn't belong in the room of couples and families, but for this brief moment, she belonged out in the night, with a man who lived the same existence that she did.

"Emma?" Astrid's footsteps sounded on the deck, and Harlan released her.

"Don't tell her I was here," he said. "I'll come by Wright's in the morning. Now is not the time." Then, without a sound, he faded into the darkness, vanishing so quickly she almost wondered whether she'd imagined him."

Sneak Peek: Darkness Possessed

An *Order of the Blade* Novel

The jungle smelled rich with the dampness of fertile soil. The trees were alive with the chatter of birds and the rustle of animals. Rhiannon closed her eyes and breathed deeply as she let the power of her birthplace roll over her and seep into her body. The freshness of the air seemed to cleanse her of all the grime and pollution that had accumulated during her years of living in civilization. She could almost feel her cells coming back to life and embracing the deep nourishment of the land she was meant to live in.

She went down on one knee and crumbled some dirt between her fingers, watching the rich, brown loam fall back to the ground from which it had come. To her surprise, she felt her throat tighten, and tears burned in her eyes. She hadn't realized how much she'd missed being home. It had been two days since she had left Boston. After much hard traveling, she'd almost reached the region that had once given her life...and then betrayed her.

A sudden sound broke through her focus and she went utterly still, listening intently. Another sound, quiet yet heavy, came from her right, and she recognized it instantly as the footstep of a creature that was too big to be a human, but could easily be a heavily armed Calydon. Without taking time to stand, she pivoted on her knee as she swept an arrow out of her quiver and pulled her crossbow off her shoulder. In less than a millisecond she nocked an arrow and had it pointing at the cluster of bushes from which the sound had come.

She knew she was in the open more than she wanted to be, but relocating into the trees would attract more attention than staying completely still. Her mottled brown and green cargo pants and jacket would help her blend into her surroundings. Even her crossbow still retained the colors of the jungle that had once been her home.

There was silence. No movement followed the steps that she had heard, which made her tension rise even further.

Whatever it was had become aware of her, and it was waiting for her to move in the same way she was anticipating its next step.

Penetrating silence prevailed, each trying to outwait the other. The muscles in her arms began to tremble, and she realized how out of shape she was. There had been a time when she had been able to hold her bow at the ready for hours, outwaiting even the most patient of enemies. Now, it had been less than a minute and already her arms were shaking. Her hamstring was cramping from the uncomfortable position she'd frozen in. A trickle of sweat was slithering down her brow, and she knew it wouldn't be long before it went into her eye. It wasn't even hot compared to what the jungle often was, but she could feel the steam rising off her body, curling her hair, and dampening her clothes.

With grim trepidation, she realized she had gone soft. She was in no condition to take on José and think she could walk away. She'd lost to him even when she'd been fit and in her prime. Now? She couldn't even hold an arrow ready for more than a minute. Her pulse began to hammer in her throat, and she willed it to quiet, knowing that José would be able to hear her heart pounding if he was the one in the bushes.

Please don't let it be José. She wasn't ready to face him yet. If she met him now, she would have no chance. A cold fear gripped her, and her fingers tightened involuntarily around the arrow, even as she fought to stay relaxed. Physical tension would throw off her aim. She had to stay loose.

Then she caught a scent, drifting to her over the complex smells of the jungle. It was the scent of a man. Not José. A stranger. He smelled of sweat, adrenaline, and something else. A deeper scent that seemed to reach inside her and unfurl in her belly. She instantly recognized her response as attraction. Desire. Lust. Dear God, *she wanted this man.* Fear gripped her with sudden cruelty, freezing her muscles and obliterating all thought from her mind except for a raw terror that screamed at her to run. *Run. Run!*

Her instincts knew she had to stay utterly still, but the fear of her attraction to a man was so deep that she could not make herself stay. Attraction was a trap. Desire could be twisted to hurt her. Lust was a cruel lie. Wanting a man was doom, torture, and a hell she'd never survive.

Instead of staying still and hidden as she should have, panic forced her to act. She leapt to her feet, spun around, and ran blindly through the forest, her boots thudding noisily on the ground. Branches tripped her and plants seemed to spring up out of the earth to grab her ankles. She couldn't even focus enough to ask them to help her instead of hurting her. Her mind was a swirling miasma of terror and memories, screaming at her to run and escape while she still had the chance.

"Hey!" The man shouted at her, his deep voice booming through the jungle.

The rich bass of his voice plunged through her flesh and ignited a fire inside her. A fire of want, longing, and the urge to turn and charge right toward him instead of away from him. "Oh, God, no. Not again." Tears streamed down her cheeks as she sprinted through the jungle, not even paying attention to where she was going. She couldn't remember the layout exactly. Her mind was fragmented with fear and terror, just as it had been so long ago when she had run for her life through these very woods. She stumbled over a root and tumbled to the earth, barely getting her hands out in time to cushion her fall. Her crossbow jammed into her jawbone and she gasped as the pain shot through her.

She hadn't even finished falling when she was already back up on her feet, stumbling as she tried to keep going. Trees loomed above her on all sides, but the branches were too high for her to reach, and she couldn't focus enough to ask the trees to help her. Everything she had as a weapon was gone, disintegrated by the fear ripping through her.

Then she realized there were heavy footsteps thundering after her, getting closer and closer. He was chasing her! She put on another burst of speed, her breath burning her lungs as she fought for air. Her legs were trembling, shaking with exhaustion as she asked her body to do things it hadn't done in so long.

She frantically tried to focus enough to take in her surroundings and understand where she was. She couldn't keep this up. She had to find a way out. She had to—

A hand closed on her shoulder, and fingers dug into her flesh, pulling her to a stop.

With his touch, all conscious thought fled from her mind. She grabbed the dagger from where it sat on her hip and spun around, striking as she turned. Her blade hit flesh, plunging deep inside thick muscle before she'd even finished her turn to see who was after her.

The dark brands on his forearms told her all she needed to know. It was a Calydon, and her dagger was in his heart. She spun the rest of the way around, facing him as he fell.

"Shit!" The warrior's dark eyes widened in surprise as he stumbled and went down to his knees.

Rhiannon ripped her dagger out of his chest and went still, bracing her legs in a ready position as she held the dagger ready. She knew she had to keep moving, but she couldn't run anymore. Not yet. She needed time to recover. She had nothing left. Her breath heaved in her chest as she desperately tried to get air.

She saw the blood pouring from his chest, and realized she'd struck a clean blow into the heart. Instinct had shown her where to find a heart on a Calydon, taking into account his height when she'd made her blind strike. Maybe she wasn't a total loss. Maybe she still had some of her old skills. Maybe she still had a chance to survive.

She took another deep breath, trying to recover from her run. She knew the respite from his injury wouldn't last long, but the heart had been a good place to hit.

He looked up at her as he pressed his palm to the wound on his chest. "Why the hell did you do that?" His voice had the same effect on her as before. It slithered through her body like a warm, seductive caress of pure temptation. And now that she could see what he looked like, it was even stronger.

His eyes were dark brown, flecked with bits of gold. His stare was intense, sinking deep into her very soul as he gazed at her. She felt herself flush under his stare, her body pulsing in response to the heat of his attention. For a moment, the world seemed to freeze, and she was caught in his spell, in his raw masculinity and strength. His cheekbones were sculpted, giving him a regal appearance, despite the heavy growth of whiskers and the disheveled dark hair, which gave him an aura of danger and lethalness that should have terrified her...but she found herself riveted by him instead.

His shoulders were broad, but not as broad as José's. Unlike José and his men, who wore camouflage pants, lean boots, and sported bare chests as if impersonating some ancient warrior, this Calydon was wearing the garb of civilization. His blue jeans were dirty and torn. His black T-shirt was loose and ragged. He was wearing hiking boots, but they appeared to be heavily insulated as if they were meant for trekking through snow and ice instead of the brutal heat of the jungle. He didn't look like he belonged to this jungle or to José, but the twin dark brands on his forearms told her all she needed to know.

He was a Calydon, and that meant he was a threat, no matter how intense her reaction to him was. In fact, he was even more dangerous *because* of the way she wanted to fall under his spell. Men knew how to take advantage of a woman's attraction to them. They preyed upon it, twisting it to their advantage. She knew better than to want a man, but her fingers actually twitched with the need to lay her hand over his wound and take away his pain, to feel his flesh beneath her palm, to move closer, and lose herself in the incredible strength and power of his being.

"Yeah…" he said softly, his gaze locked onto hers, as if he were having the same intense reaction to her that she was having to him. "Who are you?" he asked. "What's your name?"

"Who am I?" The question jerked her back to the present, to the very real danger he presented. If he'd been sent to find her, his quest would have to end now. Even as she thought it, resistance pulsed through her, and she realized she didn't want to kill him.

Grimly, she took a step back as she pulled another arrow out of her quiver. She set it in the bow and aimed it right between his eyes. "What do you want?"

She needed to know whether he had stumbled across her accidentally, or if José already knew she was here. Then, once she had her answers, she would do her best to kill the man kneeling before her.

She ignored the stab of regret at the notion of killing him. Sure, he smelled incredible and had eyes that had momentarily melted right through the fear of men that she kept wrapped so tightly around her. That didn't mean she was going to make the

same mistake that had once almost killed her. Never would she trust the wrong man, or any man, again.

Never.

He would have to die. There was simply no other option.

Select List of Other Books by Stephanie Rowe

(For a complete book list, please visit www.stephanierowe.com)

CONTEMPORARY ROMANCE

The *Wyoming Rebels* Series

A Real Cowboy Never Says No
A Real Cowboy Knows How to Kiss
A Real Cowboy Rides a Motorcycle

The *Ever After* Series

No Knight Needed
Fairytale Not Required
Prince Charming Can Wait

Stand Alone Novels

Jingle This!

PARANORMAL ROMANCE

The *NightHunter* Series

Not Quite Dead

The *Order of the Blade* Series

Darkness Awakened
Darkness Seduced
Darkness Surrendered
Forever in Darkness
Darkness Reborn
Darkness Arisen
Darkness Unleashed
Inferno of Darkness
Darkness Possessed
Shadows of Darkness
Hunt the Darkness
Release Date TBD

The *Soulfire* Series

Kiss at Your Own Risk

Touch if You Dare
Hold Me if You Can

The *Immortally Sexy* Series

Date Me Baby, One More Time
Must Love Dragons
He Loves Me, He Loves Me Hot
Sex & the Immortal Bad Boy

ROMANTIC SUSPENSE

The *Alaska Heat* Series

Ice
Chill
Ghost

NONFICTION

Essays

The Feel Good Life

FOR TEENS

A Girlfriend's Guide to Boys Series

Putting Boys on the Ledge
Studying Boys
Who Needs Boys?
Smart Boys & Fast Girls

Stand Alone Novels

The Fake Boyfriend Experiment

FOR PRE-TEENS

The *Forgotten* Series

Penelope Moonswoggle, The Girl Who Could Not Ride a Dragon
Penelope Moonswoggle & the Accidental Doppelganger
Release Date TBD

Collections

Box Sets

Alpha Immortals
Romancing the Paranormal
Last Hero Standing

Stephanie Rowe Bio

New York Times and *USA Today* bestselling author Stephanie Rowe is the author of more than 40 novels, including her popular Order of the Blade and NightHunter paranormal romance series. Stephanie is a four-time nominee of the RITA® Award, the highest award in romance fiction. She has won many awards for her novels, including the prestigious Golden Heart® Award. She has received coveted starred reviews from Booklist, and Publishers Weekly has called her work "[a] genre-twister that will make readers...rabid for more." Stephanie also writes a thrilling romantic suspense series set in Alaska. Publisher's Weekly praised the series debut, ICE, as a "thrilling entry into romantic suspense," and Fresh Fiction called ICE an "edgy, sexy and gripping thriller." Equally as intense and sexy are Stephanie's contemporary romance novels, set in the fictional town of Birch Crossing, Maine. All of Stephanie's books, regardless of the genre, deliver the same intense, passionate, and emotional experience that has delighted so many readers.

www.stephanierowe.com

http://twitter.com/stephanierowe2

http://www.pinterest.com/StephanieRowe2/

https://www.facebook.com/StephanieRoweAuthor

Made in the USA
Las Vegas, NV
31 March 2022

46635850R00125